MADE FOR YOU

Formatting and Interior Design by Bella Media Management.

First Pink Zebra Publishing Paperback Edition

ISBN-13: 978-1493765645

MADE FOR YOU

CHEYENNE MCCRAY

PINK ZEBRA PUBLISHING
SCOTTSDALE, ARIZONA

Chapter 1

Detective Reese McBride gripped two Styrofoam coffee cups as he made his way through the maze of desks toward his own. One of his hands was partially bandaged, covering the stubs of the two fingers he'd lost in an explosion, but he managed to hold on to the cup just the same.

He neared his desk that was directly across from his partner of nearly two years, Kelley Petrova. She'd been back on the job a couple of days now after sustaining a head injury and a concussion two weeks ago in the same explosion that had taken his fingers.

Kelley had transferred to the Prescott Police Department from Phoenix when she'd moved to Prescott and had been partnered with him from the start. She was beautiful, sharp, intelligent, and a damned good detective. He'd have called her cute if he didn't know her better. If anyone told her that she was cute, she'd likely kick his ass. Reese held back a smile. He could picture her doing just that.

She had a thin scar on her chin, the only thing that marred her otherwise flawless skin. Instead of detracting from her beauty, it added to it.

Ghost pains from the two missing fingers on his left hand caused him to grit his teeth. At least it was his ring finger and pinkie as opposed to his thumb, index, and middle fingers. It would be harder to be carrying coffee right now if he'd lost those three fingers in the explosion. Hell, that would have been the least of his problems. He had to admit he'd been fortunate too, in that he hadn't lost fingers on his gun hand instead of his left hand.

He studied Kelley while he managed to avoid spilling the coffee as he dodged a rookie, Brad Johnson, who hadn't been looking where he was going. Johnson apologized but Reese just grunted in response.

Reese frowned as he watched Kelley. Her pretty blue eyes looked glassy as she stared into space, appearing distracted. It was something he'd never noticed her doing before she'd sustained a concussion. The fact that she'd been injured at all made his blood boil.

It had been enormously satisfying to capture the bastard who had caused the loss of Reese's fingers and Kelley's injuries. The asshole was currently under guard in a hospital in Phoenix, having suffered third degree burns all over his body from a fire he'd set that had almost taken a woman's life. The burns were no more than he'd deserved after burning another woman to death.

Wondering if he should be even more concerned for Kelley than he already was, Reese set one of the cups of coffee in front of her before taking a big sip of his own. She seemed to be deep in thought, yet she usually did most of her thinking aloud. Of the two of them, she tended to be "shoot first, ask questions later" in a manner of speaking. However, she was a professional through and through.

He snapped his fingers in front of her face. "Snap out of it, Petrova."

Looking startled, she blinked and looked up at him. "What?"

He took his seat at his desk, facing her. "Where were you?"

She shrugged and tucked strands of her chin-length blonde hair behind her ear. "Just thinking."

He waited a moment. He'd never been one to beat around the bush, choosing to be direct when called for. "Do you think you're ready to be back at work?"

With a scowl, she straightened in her chair. "Of course I'm ready. The doctor cleared me and I'm fine."

For a moment, Reese just studied her. He'd only been cleared recently himself, but he hadn't sustained a head injury.

"Stop looking at me like that." She gave him a grumpy look. "At least let me have my coffee before you interrogate me."

A partial smile quirked at the corner of his mouth. "Some things never change." She was always a little grumpy before she had enough coffee to wire Rockefeller Center's annual Christmas tree.

"Humph." She turned to her computer screen. "We need to pay Laura Jones a visit this morning. Looks like she called in earlier and is ready to give a statement regarding Darrell Taynor, that asshole she used to call a boyfriend." Taynor had raped Laura after she broke things off with him, but they hadn't been able to get her to testify.

"Glad to hear she's finally come to her senses," Reese said.

Kelley tapped her chin. "I wonder why she didn't call me directly since we've been working her case."

"Who knows?" Reese lowered his coffee cup. "Maybe she lost your card."

"Maybe." Kelley's mouth tightened. "About time she's ready to help put that slimeball behind bars."

Reese knew his partner well enough to know that domestic violence was a sore point with her. She'd never gone into it, but his keen senses told him that in some way she'd been a victim of domestic violence. Not that she'd ever admit to being a victim in any way.

One thing about Kelley was she didn't put up with any shit. She was one of the strongest, toughest individuals he knew and that had served her well as she'd worked up the ranks in Phoenix, up to earning her detective's shield.

Reese's stepbrother and a police lieutenant, John McBride, dropped two flat rectangular boxes on top of Reese's desk. The top box had a sticker with Sweet Things Bakery on it along with the store's address.

John looked at Kelley. "You're getting too damned thin, Petrova. Need to fatten you up before someone breaks you over his knee."

Reese held back a frown. Somehow hearing another man notice Kelley's body gave him a feeling of unease, and he wasn't sure why.

"Screw you," Kelley said to John, but reached for a donut from the top box that Reese had just opened. She picked a chocolate cake donut with chocolate frosting. She bit into it and he watched her close her eyes as she tasted the chocolate flavor. Reese could tell she was holding back an appreciative moan. "Thanks, McBride," she said grudgingly to John when she opened her eyes. He smirked and moved away, leaving the boxes of donuts on Reese's desk.

Even though he didn't appreciate John noticing Kelley's figure, Reese considered telling her that John was right and she was getting too thin. He decided he'd rather not get his head snapped off first thing in the morning. He'd already practically accused her of not being ready to return to work after sustaining the concussion.

Again, the thought of the explosion that had taken his fingers and had injured Kelley made him grind his teeth. Yeah, thankfully they'd caught the sonofabitch arsonist, with his cousin Cody McBride's help, but it had cost them.

Reese picked up a donut with red, white, and blue sprinkles from Ricki's Sweet Things Bakery. He bit into the donut and had to admit it was damned good. All of his sister-in-law's treats couldn't be beat. Reese's brother, Garrett, and Ricki had married in the spring.

Other officers stopped by Reese's desk and grabbed donuts. Reese and Kelley managed to get two apiece before the two-dozen donuts were gone.

"Let's get on over to Laura Jones's place." Kelley stood and pushed in her chair. "The note said she'll be home from her late shift at Denny's any time now."

"Yep." Reese got to his feet. "Let's go."

They headed out of the police station to their unmarked car and climbed in, Reese on the passenger side. Reese and Kelley switched off when it came to driving. Both liked to drive and had come to an early compromise. This time it was her turn. Her earlier distraction flashed through his mind and he wondered if she should be driving.

He raked his fingers through his hair. Damn, he was worrying about nothing. Kelley was fine.

As she drove the radio crackled and the dispatcher gave the code for a domestic disturbance and possible shots fired, along with the address.

"That's Laura Jones's address." Kelley looked grim as she hit the lights and siren.

Reese responded to the dispatcher that they were en route.

Five minutes later they arrived at Laura's home and killed the siren. A vehicle Reese recognized as Laura's car was in the carport and a truck was in the driveway.

After Kelley parked the car, she and Reese hurried out of the vehicle and moved cautiously to the house. They unholstered their weapons, and stood to either side of the front door.

Reese banged on the door. "Police. Open up."

A woman's scream came from inside the home. Reese didn't hesitate and kicked open the door.

"We're coming in," Kelley shouted as she and Reese cleared the living room.

Another scream came from the kitchen along with a child's cry. Kelley and Reese made their way to the kitchen doorway, their weapons ready.

The scene they came upon made Reese's blood run hot then cold. Darrell Taynor had Laura on her knees, a gun pressed to her head. Taynor held his and Laura's eight-year-old daughter, Belle, with his opposite arm, a knife to her throat. The girl's blonde hair was tangled as if someone had grabbed her by her hair. Tears flooded her cheeks, her blue eyes red as she cried.

"Don't worry, Belle." Laura's voice shook but she attempted to soothe her daughter. "It's going to be okay. Everything's going to be okay, sweetheart."

"Don't come any closer." Taynor's round face was nearly purple as pressed his gun hard enough against Laura's temple that she winced. "Put your guns down or I'll shoot the bitch."

"Let her go, Darrell." Reese kept his voice calm. "This is going to end badly for you if you hurt her."

Taynor gave a nasty laugh. "Oh, it'll end up fine for me. You just better listen. Now put your guns on the floor."

"That's not going to happen and you know it." Reese kept his weapon steady. "Calm down, Darrell. Just let Laura and Belle go and you won't get hurt."

"Don't tell me to calm down," he shrieked and the girl cried out. A pinprick of blood rolled down her throat from where the blade had nicked her.

Adrenaline spiked within Reese as he saw a shadow move behind Taynor. Someone else was there. The barrel of a gun was all that Reese could see poking from the shadows. Shit. Someone he couldn't see had his gun pointed right at Kelley.

From the corner of Reese's eye he saw Kelley shift, her gun still trained on Taynor. Something wasn't right with her.

Kelley's eyes rolled back in her head and she teetered.

"I told you to put down your guns!" Taynor shrieked.

Kelley dropped to her knees.

Two shots rang out. Reese's heart thundered as Laura slumped to the floor, a hole in her temple. Reese would have taken the shot at Taynor who was still holding Belle like a shield, the knife to her throat. The gun was now near the sobbing girl's head.

A man still stood behind Taynor, his weapon still visible in the shadows.

Reese couldn't take the shot without endangering the girl.

From his side vision, Reese saw Kelley and he felt like ice-cold water had been poured over him. She had landed on her side, facing him. Blood soaked the left side of her blouse and her eyes were closed. Taynor was backing out of the door with the girl. In the next instant they and the mystery man were out of sight.

Reese crouched and put his fingers on Kelley's neck, making sure she was alive. Her pulse was strong. He did the same with Laura, whose face was away from him, against a cabinet. Judging by the hole in her head, he didn't hold much hope that she had survived. When he touched his fingers to her neck, he had no doubt she was dead.

Fury burned inside Reese. Taynor had killed Laura, and the unknown suspect had shot Kelley.

He unholstered his cell phone as he placed a call. "Officer down," he said as he rushed out the back door. Taynor, Belle, and the other man weren't in the backyard. Reese heard the sound of a truck engine starting. He ran around the side of the house to see a truck backing out of the driveway. A man was driving the truck while Taynor held his gun to Bella's head. Since the driver was on the opposite side of the cab, Reese couldn't get a good look at him. The license plate was covered with mud.

Reese hurried back into the house to Kelley, shrugging off his jacket then tearing off his shirt as fast as he could before balling it up and pressing it to her shoulder. "You're going to be fine," he said to her. "An ambulance is on its way."

She was stirring, both confusion and pain on her face as she held her hand to her left shoulder. A look of horror came across her features when she moved her hand away and saw blood on her palm—and then she glanced at Laura Jones's body.

"Oh, my God," she whispered in a gut-wrenching tone.

Kelley thought she was going to vomit as she tore her gaze from Laura's body to Reese, her stomach clenching, pain searing her shoulder. "What happened?" Her words came out in a hoarse voice. "I passed out and then I was shot?" she asked even though she already knew the answer—her mind just didn't want to process it.

Reese looked grim as he pressed his shirt to her shoulder. He checked the back of her shoulder and she held in a cry of pain. "Looks like the bullet went through."

He asked her a few questions that she knew were designed to make sure she was coherent. Impatiently, horror growing inside her, she brushed his questions aside.

Guilt stabbed her chest like knives. "Laura's dead and Belle is gone." Disbelief and loss of blood made Kelley feel lightheaded, even as she stared at Laura's body. She heard sirens as she tore her gaze away and looked at Reese. "It was my fault."

"Don't start thinking that way, Kelley." He rarely used her first name when talking with her—he normally addressed her as Petrova and she called him McBride. "Taynor was on the edge. He had every intention of killing Laura Jones and taking the girl." She saw his jaw clench. "I think the shot that hit you came from a man behind Taynor."

"I saw him right before I blacked out." Kelley never cried but she felt heat and a harsh prickle at the backs of her eyes as she gritted her teeth from the pain in her shoulder. She'd never been shot before. She struggled to get ahold of herself. "If I hadn't passed out—"

"Laura would have been killed regardless," Reese said.

Sirens sounded in the distance as she said, "You're full of shit, you know that, Reese? It was my fault." Just like when her father killed her mother, it was her fault for not being there when she should have been.

This time she'd passed out and hadn't been there to save Laura.

"Don't blame yourself, damn it." Reese helped prop her against a wall as she insisted on struggling to sit rather than remaining on the floor. "It was *not* your fault."

She was disgusted to find that her head was spinning. She tried pushing him away with her good hand and looked at Laura. Kelley didn't know why she bothered, considering the hole in Laura's head and her pale, still body, but nevertheless she asked, "Are you sure she's dead?"

His mouth was in a thin tight line. "Yes."

Kelley struggled not to cry out from the pain in her shoulder as she looked at Reese. Her mind was confused, battling between her guilt and all that she had in her life that mattered anymore. "I don't know anything but being a cop." She heard the strain in her own voice. "Now I've gone and fucked up big time. What the hell do I do?"

"No one needs to know you passed out," Reese said quietly. "Taynor shot Laura and at the same time you were shot by an unknown suspect."

She shook her head, a leaden weight on her chest. She opened her mouth to speak but Reese spoke over her.

"You know what happened," he said slowly as cruisers and ambulances pulled up to the front of the house and cut their sirens, lights flashing through the windows. "Taynor held Belle and Laura hostage with a second suspect backing him up. Then the unknown suspect shot you while Taynor shot the victim and escaped with the girl. There was nothing either of us could have done without the chance that Taynor would hurt the girl. You know that's what happened."

Kelley stared at Reese. "But if I hadn't passed out," she said again, this time finishing what she'd tried to say earlier, "Laura would be alive and Belle would still be here."

His mouth tightened. "This isn't the time to do what you might consider to be the noble thing. Just keep to the story and you'll go to the hospital and take time off. That's all you need to do." When she didn't answer he narrowed his eyes. His voice was almost harsh as he said, "Understand, Petrova?"

Feeling mute, she nodded as she heard John McBride's voice coming from the front door.

"Taynor's long gone," Reese called out. "We've got a body in here."

Referring to Laura Jones as a body caused bile to rise up in Kelley's throat. She'd seen plenty of dead bodies in her career, but this one was far worse. She'd been responsible. She swallowed. If she hadn't passed out, Laura would still be alive.

Kelley bowed her head. Just like her mother would still be alive if Kelley had been there for her.

In the next moment, paramedics were attending to Kelley. She remained mute, pain gripping her as Reese ran through his version of what had happened. She felt weaker and weaker, and it really pissed her off.

An Amber Alert had been issued and locally everyone and their mother had received the alert on their cell phones and it had already been broadcast on radio and television. The alert included the make and model of the truck, Taynor's name, age, and appearance as well as the missing child's, and that a second suspect had been seen but remained unidentified.

When John turned away to speak with other officers on the scene, Reese knelt beside Kelley again and looked into her eyes. "Are you okay?"

She swallowed. "I'll be fine."

As the paramedics prepared to put Kelley on the gurney, Reese brushed hair from her face. "I'm going to go with you to the hospital."

Despite the pain in her arm and the spinning in her head, she didn't want to go to the hospital. She wanted to do something to find Laura's killer and her daughter, and the second suspect who'd helped Taynor get away.

She didn't have to say a word—Reese knew her too well. He shook his head. "I know you'll want to help when you're out of the hospital, but you've got to get it through your head that you'll need to recover from the bullet wound and the concussion."

As far as the concussion, Kelley had known something wasn't quite right. She hadn't been feeling well, but she'd pushed it aside, certain that she'd be able to function just fine. How wrong she'd been.

Again pressure built up behind her eyes. Old feelings and memories that she'd thought had been long buried rose up inside her. She clenched her hands into fists and took a deep breath and then another one. She had to get herself under control. Had to.

"How bad are you hurt, Petrova?" John McBride stood beside her as the paramedics put her on the gurney.

She was feeling weaker and weaker. "I'll live," she muttered.

John frowned. "Something's wrong, and I'm not talking about the bullet you took in the shoulder."

He had always been perceptive with a keen cop sense. She thought about telling him the truth but held it back. Reese was putting his own career on the line by lying to cover up her mistake. The least she could do was keep to his story. "I got shot. What the hell else do you think it could be?"

John just studied her. "Take care of yourself."

Kelley didn't answer. Instead she fought back tears she refused to cry.

CHAPTER 2

"I'm fine." Kelley's voice traveled down the hospital corridor as Reese walked in that direction. "I want to go home," she demanded. "And I don't need any more damned morphine."

"You're not going anywhere until the doctor releases you," came a no-nonsense female reply as Reese reached Kelley's room. "The doctor already told you that you need to stay until he feels you're well enough to leave," the nurse added as Reese entered the doorway.

When he saw Kelley, his gut twisted. The normally tough spitfire of a detective appeared so pale, almost delicate, propped up against the white pillows, an IV attached to the back of her hand. Despite her weak appearance, she still looked mulish as she glared at the nurse.

"Let me have a little chat with Detective Petrova," Reese said to the pretty dark-haired nurse named Nancy, who he'd met on an earlier visit. She somehow managed to look calm in spite of Kelley's stubbornness.

The nurse faced him, her back to Kelley, and gave a little smile. "She's all yours, Detective McBride. Just see that she keeps her butt in bed."

Reese winked at Nancy. "You bet."

When the nurse left the room, Kelley glared at him. "I don't need to be here. I can rest up just as well at home."

"You, rest?" He snorted. "I think you belong right here as long as they'll keep you."

"Humph." Kelley started to cross her arms over her chest then winced, pain flashing across her face. Still, she did not make a sound even though it clearly hurt her to move.

Guilt stabbed Reese's insides like a knife. He'd seen that Kelley was still affected by the concussion, but he'd let her go with him to Laura Jones's place. If he'd just insisted that she wasn't ready—

Even as he berated himself, he knew that it wouldn't have done a damned bit of good. Kelley would have gone anyway.

But couldn't he have done something to keep her from being shot?

He pulled up a chair beside her bed. The colorful bouquet of flowers he'd brought her earlier was on a stand next to the bed with the card beside it. "How are you really doing, Kelley?"

The stubborn look faded. "I'm fine. I should be home. I should be—"

He cut across her words. "Don't say you should be looking for that bastard, Taynor." Reese frowned. "You leave that up to Prescott's finest."

She let out her breath. He knew she wouldn't argue that the men and women of PPD were good at their jobs. Still, she said, "But one more person searching for him will bring us that much closer." She sounded as if she might cry as she said. "I have to do this."

"What can you do with that shoulder?" Reese said quietly. "Not to mention you're going to have to go through physical therapy."

Kelley frowned. "Like I have time for that."

"You'll have plenty of time while you're on leave. You know you need PT if you're going to get back to a hundred percent." He reached out and put his hand over hers. "Take it easy, okay? Promise me?"

She looked at his hand covering hers and something he couldn't define made his heart thump a little faster. When her eyes met his, she had an almost surprised look, as if she had felt something, too.

He squeezed her hand. "Promise me."

Her throat worked as she swallowed. "I can't."

"Damn it, Petrova." He moved his hand from hers. "You're going to make things worse with your shoulder if you're not careful. If that happens, it will be even longer before you'll be back to full speed."

If he didn't know better, he'd think she was holding back tears. Kelley's jaw visibly tightened. He knew that on the occasions Kelley had met with Laura, Kelley had had the opportunity to talk with Belle

"He's out there," Kelley said. "He killed Laura and he has her daughter. I owe it to Laura to help put the bastard behind bars and get her daughter back safely." She clenched the fist he'd just touched. "For God's sake, Belle is only eight."

Reese dragged his palm down his face. The ghost pains from his missing fingers made his whole hand throb. "I'm on it. I will find them."

Kelley looked away and stared out the window. Again she looked like she might be holding back tears. After a long moment, she turned back to face him. "Find the bastard," she said, a fierceness in her voice.

"I will." He put his hand over hers. "You can count on it."

Warmth so deep touched Kelley clear to her soul. She'd worked with Reese for almost two years and she'd never experienced anything like this before. She cared for him, would give her life for his, but this was something more.

Had it always been there? Or was she feeling it now because of the fact that she had come so close to death? A couple of inches to the right and the bullet would have entered her heart. Was that why she had these crazy feelings inside her for Reese that she couldn't control?

Or it could be the fact that her brain was addled with morphine even though the effects were starting to wear off and pain was shooting through her shoulder. Still, maybe the residual morphine was the cause of these funny feelings she was having around Reese.

He released her hand and she immediately missed his touch. "I'll head down to the station and get to work finding Taynor," Reese said. "Your job is to get better. Understand?"

She didn't want to give in. It wasn't in her nature to sit on the sidelines and not be a part of something so important. And finding Taynor and his daughter were more than important. It could even mean the little girl's life or death.

"Yeah," she finally said. "But when I get out of here—"

"You're going to work on healing and getting into form," he said, cutting across her words. "I want my partner back." He squeezed her hand one last time before letting go. "I'll see you again before you're released."

"I don't plan on being here that long," she muttered.

He smiled and met her gaze for one long last look. His light brown hair was a little out of place and he had a day's stubble on his jaws. His vivid blue eyes held hers and she didn't think he'd ever looked more handsome than he did at that moment. He was muscular with an athlete's build and he filled out the T-shirt he was wearing in a way that made her heart pattering harder.

It had to be the morphine. She mentally shook her head as he turned away and headed out the door. She watched him as he left, feeling strangely bereft without him there.

She sank against the pillows and looked at the ceiling. Being in the hospital with this injury was definitely addling her brain. Of course she would feel something for her partner after all this time, and not in a romantic way. She cared about him as much as she did because of all they'd been through together. This was just another facet of their partnership. They had been through a lot.

And now this… She was barely conscious of rubbing the pale thin scar on her chin as everything whirled through her mind. She hated this helpless feeling when she should be out there chasing after a murdering bastard, where she belonged.

Men who treated women as less than equals infuriated her. But men who hurt women, men who killed women, put her into a rage so great that she knew she had to keep a tight rein on herself. After what her father did to her and her mother—

Before she could stop them, memories of the past flashed through her mind.

Her mother's screams and Kelley's own cries rang in her ears…from the time she was a little girl until she ran away from home as a teenager, her father had beaten both of them. Memories assaulted her of all of the tears she'd cried as she'd watched her mother being knocked around by her father…and then how her father had whipped Kelley with a belt when her mother wasn't there to take her father's punches.

When he wasn't beating them, he would tell them how worthless they were. He'd say a woman's only uses were to have babies, and to cook for and clean up after men.

Isaac Petrova had been more than a bastard. He'd been evil. She'd hated him more than she'd hated anyone in her life. She had never stopped hating him.

She buried her face in her hands, even as pain shot through her from moving her shoulder. Her skin felt hot and tight.

Guilt weighed heavily on her soul. Kelley's father had killed her mother not long after Kelley had run away from home when she was sixteen. If she'd been there or had done something to stop him, her mother might still be alive. But Kelley wondered if she'd be dead just like her mother if she'd stayed around.

Isaac Petrova was in prison for his wife's death. Kelley had never been to visit him and never would. He would rot there.

God, how she missed her mother. Kelley felt a hot tear at the corner of her eye and brushed it away impatiently. She didn't cry, damn it. Long ago she'd promised herself she'd never cry again and that she would never, ever be a victim.

Instead, she fought to uplift and protect women and volunteered at women's shelters when she could. She had worked hard to succeed in a male-dominated career and had made a place for herself.

She leaned back against the pillows, frustration making her entire body tense and her shoulder throb even more. She didn't consider herself to be a victim in any way. Belle and Laura were the victims.

Kelley gripped the hand of her good arm into a fist. When she got out of this damned hospital, she'd do what she could from home until she was stronger. Hopefully it wouldn't be that long before Taynor and Belle were found, and Kelley wanted to find whomever it was that had shot her, too. One thing she refused to do was sit around and let that bastard get away with the little girl.

Nancy walked in holding a syringe. "I need to give you another dose of morphine, Detective."

"I said no." Kelley shook her head and clenched her jaw as she tried not to cry out from the pain it caused when she made the movement. "I don't need it."

With a sigh, Nancy said, "You cops are all the same. Too damned stubborn for your own good."

Kelley felt like snapping at Nancy, but the nurse was only doing her job. Kelley knew she shouldn't take out her frustrations on the woman.

She let out her breath. "I'm sorry, but I'm a little wound up right now."

Nancy smiled. "So you'll take the morphine?"

Kelley shook her head. "The only thing that will make me feel any better is getting the hell out of this place."

"That's not going to happen today." Nancy started to leave the room then looked over her shoulder as she paused in the doorway. "Get some rest, Detective. The more you rest, the sooner your body will heal." The nurse turned away again and left the room.

Kelley let out a rush of breath. She had to admit that she wasn't a very good patient. She'd only recently been cleared to go back to work from the head injury and concussion. For some reason the back of her head ached where the stitches had been.

Here she was, right back where she'd been a couple of weeks ago. She'd been lucky in both instances. She could have died as a result of the explosion, or she could have died this morning when the man had shot her.

She narrowed her eyes as she thought of Taynor and his accomplice. She prayed Reese and the men and women in blue would find the bastard and the little girl soon. If they didn't, come hell or high water, Kelley would.

* * * * *

After yet another dead-end lead, Reese ground his teeth. He was determined to find Taynor and Belle. Not only for the little girl's sake, but for Kelley, too. Finding the man who'd shot Kelley was top on Reese's list, too.

He leaned back in his seat at his desk that faced Kelley's. He hated seeing her chair empty and would have liked nothing more than to have her there right now.

The thought of how close Kelley had come to death was a knife to his gut. He didn't know what he'd do if something happened to her. She wasn't just his partner—

He frowned and picked up a pen from his desk and fiddled with it. What was Kelley if she wasn't just his partner? He thought about that moment in the hospital when he'd touched her and the crazy feelings that had gone through him. From her expression, she'd felt it, too.

His frown deepened and he started tapping the pen on a pad of paper on his desk. He wasn't too sure he wanted to explore those feelings right now.

He scanned the computer screen, looking over the leads from the Amber Alert. He'd gone through them time and again. All of the leads were being followed up on, but none of them had panned out so far. He'd been out to investigate the strongest leads himself. He gritted his teeth and barely kept from snapping the pen he was gripping and tossed it back onto the desk instead.

Something about this case hit close to home with Kelley and Reese wondered why. He'd noticed that most cases involving domestic violence against a woman or child set Kelley off. It was beyond her being passionate about her job. Something about this one was even worse for Kelley.

The more he thought about it, the more his keen investigative senses made him want to learn more. He wanted to know what made Kelley Petrova so passionate about her work… Exactly what made her tick?

A part of him knew he shouldn't invade her privacy in that way, but the part that wanted to know won out.

He searched through the police database and came up with Kelley's file. He felt a moment's guilt, but pushed it aside. As he read the file his mouth tightened into a thin line. Kelley's mother was deceased and her father was in prison. The file didn't tell him a whole lot more.

Reese opened up an Internet browser and typed in her father's name, Isaac Petrova and her mother's name, Jill Petrova. He had to sort through various hits, but finally found old articles dating back fifteen years ago when Kelley would have been sixteen.

As he read through the articles, Reese's brows narrowed. Isaac Petrova had been found guilty of murdering his wife, Jill. They'd had one daughter but her name had not been released as she had been a minor at the time.

The article told of the brutal murder where Isaac had bludgeoned his wife to death and that he had abused his minor child.

Reese's gut clenched. The shock that went through him wasn't just because of what had happened to her mother and the fact that her father had beat them both. It was because his story was eerily familiar to hers. What were the odds that they'd been through such similar things as they grew up?

What had happened to Kelley was enough to make her as passionate as she was about seeing that justice was served when it came to domestic violence. That was in line with how he felt, too, after his own upbringing.

When he thought about what Kelley had gone through, he found himself wanting to beat the shit out of Isaac Petrova. If the man hadn't been in prison, Reese would have wanted to track him down and do it himself.

He closed out the browser and went back to checking up on leads for the Taynor case. Something had to break and soon.

CHAPTER 3

Kelley stood in her kitchen, glad to be home even though it would be some time yet before the doctor cleared her to go back to work. A couple of days in the hospital had nearly driven her out of her mind.

Now that she was back, she would figure out what she could do from home to find Taynor and Belle. Kelley shook her head. How had he eluded the police so well?

She rubbed her temples. She was exhausted from the little sleep she'd had. Every time she closed her eyes, she saw Laura's body…and Belle's, too.

And then there were the nightmares.

Laura's funeral had been yesterday. The fact that Belle's birth father had murdered her mother hit so close to home that Kelley felt almost shattered from it. It was all she could do not to let it affect her in a way that might cripple her ability to do her job and find Laura's killer.

Kelley's phone rang. Since her right arm was in a sling, she had to pull the phone out of her pocket with her left hand and she almost dropped the device. She looked at the number and scowled. Her grandmother again—she'd called twice while Kelley was in the hospital. She had no desire to speak to her paternal grandmother, so she pressed the button to send the call to voicemail and then pocketed the phone again. Dolores Petrova lived in Phoenix, which wasn't far enough away as far as Kelley was concerned.

The fact that her father's mother had been calling made Kelley think about the past, something she tried not to do. She wandered into her sparsely furnished living room. She'd never been much of a decorator or creature of comfort. She wasn't a homebody or a collector, and she only had one memento of her childhood—with the exception of the scar.

She moved to an end table and used her left hand to pick up the Christmas globe that Kelley's mother had given her when she was five. The scene inside the snow globe was of Santa and a sleigh with nine tiny reindeer pulling it. Rudolph was in the lead with his shiny red nose.

Kelley smiled wistfully at the globe that reminded her of the times she and her mother had spent together, while Isaac was at work. Every Christmas, Jill would find a moment to give Kelley a snow globe when they were alone. Over the years, Kelley had accumulated quite a collection and had kept them hidden from her father.

Now and then, when the house was quiet and Isaac had drunk himself into a stupor, Kelley would get out the snow globes and dream of visiting the magical places inside the globes. Some were Christmas scenes, others with characters and lands from fairytales. The globes had included Cinderella and her prince next to the pumpkin coach, the Little Mermaid under the sea, Belle and her Beast, and several others.

Those were all gone now with the exception of the very first one, which Isaac hadn't found. He had discovered her hiding place and had thrown all of the other globes at the wall. He had shattered them, leaving her in tears while she cleaned up the broken pieces and the destroyed worlds.

She gripped the snow globe she was holding so tightly her knuckles hurt. Her mother had been a kind and gentle person who had been taken in by Isaac and his charm. He'd wooed her with flowers and other romantic gestures, until she married him. They weren't too far into their marriage before he'd started abusing her.

The only time Isaac hadn't beaten Jill had been when she was pregnant because he'd been so sure they would have a son. Not long after Kelley was born, he started beating Jill again, blaming her for not giving him a boy. He didn't start abusing Kelley until she was five, and even then he always made sure the bruises were out of sight.

For a long time, Kelley had blamed her mother for not leaving Isaac. But Jill had felt trapped. She hadn't gone to college, had never worked, had no money, and no way to support her daughter.

Kelley closed her eyes tightly before opening them again, and carefully set the snow globe down beside the others. Collecting them had been a way of remembering her mother. Kelley purchased a globe every Christmas that reminded her of one of her mother had given her.

The doorbell rang, catching Kelley off guard. She wasn't expecting anyone—unless Nikki was early, and Nikki was *never* early. As it was, Kelley always had to tell her friend to pick her up twenty minutes earlier than she really needed to leave, so she knew it couldn't be her.

Kelley glanced at the entryway table. She kept her Glock in a drawer in the table when she wasn't carrying the weapon. She wasn't as good left-handed as she was using her right, but she could still do a damned good job of protecting herself if she needed to.

She moved quietly to the door and peeked out the peephole. Shocked, she drew back, feeling a mixture of surprise, pain, and anger so hot it felt as if her skin might burn off. What was *she* doing here?

Gritting her teeth, she unlocked the doorknob followed by the bolt lock, and jerked the door open. For a long moment she and the sharply dressed older woman stared at each other.

"Aren't you going to tell your grandmother hello?" Dolores Petrova said in a disapproving tone.

Kelley tried to school her expression but no doubt it looked as hard and angry as she felt. "Why are you here, dear grandmother?"

Dolores gave a pained smile. "Invite me in and I'll tell you why I'm here."

Kelley scowled but opened the door wide enough to let her grandmother in. Kelley wasn't in the mood for Dolores to make a scene in front of her neighbors. The older woman was good at making scenes.

After closing the door behind Dolores, Kelley stood in the middle of the living room and clenched the hand of her good arm into a fist. Her shoulder ached from the tension in her whole body. "Why did you come here without an invitation?"

"If you'd answer your phone, you'd know," Dolores said dryly.

Kelley ignored the response. "What do you want?"

Dolores brushed an imaginary piece of lint off the tailored jacket of her expensive taupe business suit and schooled her tone. "Is that any way to talk to your grandmother?"

"You haven't been my grandmother for fifteen years." Kelley was having a difficult time controlling her temper. "What do you want?" she repeated.

Dolores tilted her chin. "Your father is dying from lung cancer."

A confusion of feelings came over Kelley, shock being the strongest. "So?" she finally said. "Is that supposed to mean something to me?"

"He's your father," Dolores snapped, some of her cool slipping.

"I don't have a father." Kelley's jaw tightened. "As far as I'm concerned, it's a shame that man is dying only because I'd like to see him rot for eternity in that prison."

Dolores's face seemed to whiten. "You're a stupid girl, just like your mother was."

Kelley clenched her free hand into a fist. "Don't you dare talk about my mother."

The older woman gave a sniff. "You know your father didn't kill her and you lied about him hitting you."

"You can leave now." Kelley pointed toward the door. "I don't even know why you bothered to come here."

"You should see your father before he passes away." Dolores's gray eyes were like flint. "And beg his forgiveness."

Kelley's jaw dropped. "You're serious? You want me to beg forgiveness from that monster who killed my mother and physically abused me?"

"Still lying, I see." Dolores narrowed her eyes. "I thought perhaps you would feel some guilt for what you did to Isaac. You're just as delusional as you always were."

"Get out." Kelley struggled to calm herself and knew she was losing the battle. "And don't ever come back."

Kelley grabbed the door handle with her good hand and jerked the door open. "Go," she said, her whole body taut with anger. "Don't bother to ever come back. *Ever.*"

Dolores raised her chin. When she stood in the doorway, she paused to look down her nose at Kelley. "You're just as bad as your mother was."

Kelley barely kept from slamming the door into her grandmother's face. It took every bit of her control to not say anything and shut the door quietly but firmly behind Dolores. She turned around, looking for something to throw. Instead, she grabbed a throw pillow off the couch, buried her face against it, and screamed her fury.

When she dropped the pillow, she didn't feel any better. No, she needed to shoot something. *That* would make her feel better. A whole hell of a lot better. She had a couple of paper targets at the shooting range with her father's and grandmother's names on them.

By the time the doorbell rang again, Kelley was so worked up that she was wishing she had taken a quick jog on her treadmill. The only thing that had stopped her was the pain in her shoulder.

Nikki Carlyle was on the doorstep, Kelley's closest friend. Nikki frowned when she saw Kelley's expression. "Are you all right?"

Kelley pinched the bridge of nose with her thumb and forefinger. She took a deep breath then let it out slowly. When she looked at her friend she managed a strained smile. "Yeah, fine. Just had an unwelcome visitor."

Nikki was still frowning. "Want to talk about it?"

Kelley shook her head. "I might kill something or someone if I talk about it now."

"Okay." Nikki offered Kelley a supportive smile. Nikki was the opposite of Kelley in so many ways. Nikki was tall and dark-haired while Kelley was petite and blonde. Kelley wasn't trusting, not very social, didn't date much, and kept mostly to herself. Nikki, on the other hand, was sanguine, what one would call a social butterfly, and a heartbreaker on top of that. She didn't break hearts on purpose—her ADHD personality just made it difficult for one man to keep her attention for very long.

Nikki shook back her long dark hair. "Let's get you to your physical therapy appointment."

With a groan, Kelley said, "The PT appointment went straight out of my mind. Let me grab my purse and my phone." She hadn't been cleared for driving and Nikki had insisted on getting Kelley back and forth to PT as often as she could. Nikki owned an elegant antique store on Gurley and her schedule was flexible. Kelley hadn't wanted to impose, but Nikki had insisted, and she definitely could be persistent.

A few moments later and they were climbing into Nikki's sporty little two-seater BMW. Her wealthy father had given it to her for her birthday—he gave Nikki all a girl could ever want and then some. She admitted to being spoiled, but she was a sweetheart and Kelley liked everything about her.

The entire trip to the physical therapy office, Nikki talked while Kelley quietly seethed over her grandmother's visit. Nikki's enthusiastic chatter meant that Kelley didn't have to do much talking, and she was grateful for that.

When they reached the PT office, Nikki said, "I'm going to run a couple of errands and stop by the store. Call me when you're ready for me to pick you up." She got out and hurried to the passenger side of the low-slung car as Kelley tried to climb out one-handed. Grudgingly, Kelley took Nikki's hand, allowing her friend to help her out. She scowled. She hated being helpless in any way.

Damn it, she was *not* helpless.

By the time she reached the physical therapy office, she was worked up about her grandmother's visit, with no outlet. She was afraid she was going to blow up. She waved goodbye to Nikki and headed into the office.

"You'll be working with Johan," the PT director introduced her to a tall, muscular blond man who looked and sounded Swedish when he spoke. He was one gorgeous hunk of male.

"How is your day, Kelley?" Johan asked as they walked into the little gym used for physical therapy. "You look as if something is bothering you."

Kelley gritted her teeth. "You don't want to know."

"Try me." He grinned as he helped her take off her sling. "Talking with your physical therapist is like talking to a bartender. It is good."

She shook her head. "That's one I've never heard before."

He began her therapy session by asking questions about her injury before moving her arm and finding out what she could do now and what she needed to work up to.

Two other therapists were working with clients while Johan worked with Kelley. He showed her exercises and then had her do each exercise in sets. Some of them hurt but she was determined to do everything. The sooner she got her arm back to full strength, the better.

As he worked with her, she learned that he had come from Sweden alone when he was twelve to stay with an uncle in Prescott after his parents died in small plane crash. He worked hard in school, excelled at American football, and got a full ride scholarship to Arizona State University for football after he'd graduated from high school.

His second year at ASU he'd had a career-ending injury. After having worked with physical therapists to recover from his injury, he'd decided to become a physical therapist to help people in the same situation as his—people whose dreams had been interrupted or altered thanks to a life-changing injury.

As he told her about his own background, he got Kelley to tell him a little bit about her childhood. Surprisingly, she was finding that it wasn't hard to open up to him.

"Ten times," he instructed her as he showed her another exercise to strengthen her shoulder. "Now why don't you tell me?" he said once she started the exercise.

She grimaced as her shoulder ached from the movement as she did the exercise. "Tell you what?"

He met her gaze. He had kind eyes. She was an excellent judge of character, and she could tell he genuinely cared as he asked the question. "Why were you upset when you arrived?"

She thought about it for a moment. What would it hurt to tell him? He had nothing to do with her line of work and it wasn't like she would be seeing him anywhere outside of physical therapy.

And considering she refused to see a shrink or other therapist, maybe it would help to get it out to someone who was impartial.

"Well," she said slowly, "the grandmother from hell showed up on my doorstep today."

"That bad?" he said.

Kelley nodded. "Worse."

"Tell me about it," he said as he showed her another exercise.

She sighed. "It's a long and not so nice story."

"Go on."

She found herself telling him about her grandmother's visit from the moment she arrived until Kelley made her leave, and about her father, too. Johan felt safe…and so far removed from her everyday life that it wouldn't matter how he looked at her after telling him. He was right—it was a little like telling a bartender her woes.

As they did the exercises and she told him about her grandmother and father, he didn't look at her with pity and she didn't sense that he thought any differently of her than he would have when she walked in the front door, and he didn't see her as emotionally weak. There was sympathy and understanding, yes, but not pity. He asked her questions as she told him of her past, but his questions didn't feel intrusive.

To her surprise, after talking with Johan her heart felt lighter and she felt more able to process her anger about what had happened with her grandmother.

"Thank you for your point of view and the conversation," she said with a smile.

"My pleasure." He smiled at her in return. "Now let me show you a couple of relaxation exercises that will help clear your mind and help you deal with some of the chaotic thoughts and feelings you have going on inside."

He was remarkably intuitive and had great bedside manner.

When they finished with the exercises, she was sore as Johan put his arm around her shoulders. She smiled up at him as he walked with her out to the waiting room to find Reese watching and waiting.

CHAPTER 4

"I will see you the day after tomorrow, same time, yes?" Johan asked.

Kelley nodded. "As long as I can get a ride, I'll be here."

"She'll have a ride." Reese stood up and moved to her side. "I'll make sure of it."

For some reason, Kelley felt like she needed to explain why Johan had his arm around her shoulders. She slipped out from under his hold and smiled. "Johan, this is my partner, Detective McBride." To Reese she said, "This is Johan, my physical therapist."

Johan grinned and held out his hand. Reese took it and gave a nod.

"I'm expecting another client soon." Johan smiled at Kelley. "Do your exercises at home and try the meditation on your own, too."

"I will." She returned his smile. She already felt like they were old friends, something she rarely if ever felt with people she'd just met.

Johan turned and walked back into the physical therapy room and Kelley looked at Reese. He was so much taller than her—almost a foot over her five-two—that she had to look up at him.

She found herself frowning. "What are you doing here? Nikki is supposed to pick me up."

Reese gave a nod toward the front entrance. "Sorry to disappoint you, but I offered to take you home when I ran into Nikki downtown. She had a little crisis at her store."

Kelley felt a little chagrined as they walked into the late afternoon sunshine. "Not that I'm not appreciative, it's just that I didn't expect you."

They reached Reese's truck that was parked in a spot directly in front of the entrance and he unlocked the door. "I told her I was planning on coming to see you this evening anyway."

"Oh?" Kelley let him help her up into the cab of the truck. "You were?"

"Yep," he said before closing the passenger door and she waited for him to go around to the driver's side.

Once he'd climbed in and settled himself into the driver's seat, she said, "Why?"

He looked amused. "Can't I come see my partner when she's out of commission?"

She couldn't help a smile at his little grin. "Of course."

"How was PT?" he asked as he drove toward her home.

She tried to shrug but it hurt her shoulder so she said, "It was okay."

"You don't have to act tough." He put on his blinker before he turned the truck turned left at an intersection. "I already know you are."

"I'm not acting tough." She looked out the window. Hell if she'd complain about it being painful to use her arm in the exercises. It was true that she didn't like the perception of being weak in any way. "It was fine."

When she glanced back at him, he was concentrating on the road. He looked like he had something on his mind.

She tilted her head to the side. "What's up with you?"

"I hope you like tortellini." He pulled his truck up to her house and killed the engine. He clearly was changing the subject this time. "Because that's what you're getting for dinner."

"Oh, yeah?" She raised her brows.

He nodded. "That's right."

She shook her head as he jumped out of the truck and went around to her side to help her out. He had a chivalrous cowboy nature, but when they worked together he never tried to open a car door for her. Doing that in her line of work would have undermined her authority as a cop.

After she was out of the truck, he grabbed two big grocery bags then locked his truck and walked with her up to her front door.

She unlocked it, stepped inside, and held the door open for him. "What's in the bags?"

"You'll see soon enough." He walked in and headed toward the kitchen while she shut the front door.

She followed him, curious, and he set the bags on the counter. She peered into one bag as he emptied the other. Two packages of fresh cheese and spinach tortellini, grated Parmesan cheese, a big onion, a garlic bulb, a stick of butter, fresh basil, and a small carton of half-and-half. Out of the other bag he produced a loaf of

French bread, a package of pre-made salad along with tomatoes, a bottle of bleu cheese dressing, a can of chicken broth, a box of corn starch, a can of black olives, and a small chocolate cake with chocolate Ganache icing.

"You know how much I love chocolate." She felt better just looking at all that yummy chocolate icing. "You'd already won me over even without the tortellini, but now you're my favorite person in the universe."

"For today." He gave her a quick smile as he emptied the sack she'd been looking in. "I know the way to your heart, Petrova."

It wasn't long before water was boiling on the stove and the house was filled with the delicious smells of garlic and onion sizzling in a pan. She watched him move efficiently around the kitchen. The fact that he was missing two fingers didn't seem to affect him, or at least he didn't show it if it did.

As she watched him, a warm squishy sensation went through her belly that she'd never felt before with anyone. Ever. Tall and muscular, he looked so damned good, standing there in front of her stove. She studied his profile, his hard but handsome features, his well-cut and defined biceps and triceps, and the way his T-shirt molded to his impressive physique. His Wrangler jeans showed what a nice ass he had. It was hard not to love a cowboy in Wranglers.

Reese looked a lot different from John, his brother. John was a good-looking man but tended to be more serious and rarely smiled. Reese, though, had a smile that was sexy as hell.

Yes, she had to admit he was one of the sexiest men she'd ever met. When she first started working for the Prescott Police Department, she'd made a point of *not* noticing how attractive any man might be on the force. Okay, she'd noticed, but had kept thoughts like that out of her mind. She'd been determined to make her way in a man's world without anyone thinking she was sleeping her way to the top. She'd kept her distance and kept things professional.

Pushing thoughts of sexy partners aside, she peered around the big man's shoulder. "What are you making?"

He stirred the ingredients he'd put into the pan. "A garlic cream sauce to go with the tortellini."

"All this time we've been working together and I had no idea you know how cook like this," she said. "I'm impressed. That's definitely one thing we don't have in common." She pointed toward her phone. "My dinners are always on speed dial."

"I figured as much." He gave a low chuckle. "In a town this size, you can't have a lot of options."

"I live on a lot of pizza." She leaned up against a counter. "Where did you learn how to cook?"

"My mom." He added half-and-half, broth, and cornstarch to the mixture in the pan. "She made me and my brother, and my stepbrothers, learn how to cook."

"My mother tried to teach me." Kelley gave a rueful smile. "But I never had an interest in it." Kelley felt an instant weight on her chest and she didn't know why it came out, but she said, "Now she's not around to teach me anything. She's in a cemetery in Phoenix."

He glanced up from cooking. He looked intent but not surprised. "I'm sorry."

Kelley looked away from him but for some reason she felt like talking. "My father used to beat me and my mom." She touched the thin scar on her chin. "After I ran away from home, he beat her to death. The bastard is in prison now."

"Is that where you got the scar?" he asked as he watched her fingers tracing it. He reached up with his index finger and ran it along the scar, too.

She let her hand drop away from her face. "Yes."

Reese was quiet for a moment then said, "We have a lot in common. Both of our fathers abused us and both are convicts."

Kelley looked at him in surprise. "Your father is in prison?"

Reese gave a nod. "My father used to physically abuse my mother, my brother, and me. He did it for fun. Fortunately, we got away and Mom took my brother and me to a shelter. The old man's been in prison for a while for having sex with a minor."

"At least your mom was smart enough to get you away from your father." Kelley shook her head. "No, that's not fair. My mom was sweet and gentle. She was raised to believe you stuck with marriage through good and bad. And she didn't have the first idea what she'd do if she left him."

"I'm sorry you went through all that you did," Reese said.

"I miss her," Kelley said quietly. "All I have left of her is a snow globe she gave me when I was a child."

"You collect them?" he asked.

She shrugged and changed the subject. "So you're not a McBride from birth?" she asked.

"Nope." He shook his head. "My mom married my stepdad, Hal, and he legally adopted Garrett and me. John and Mike are our stepbrothers."

"That's why you look so much different than John and Mike." Kelley tilted her head to the side. "How odd we both have such similar stories."

"It's probably why we're doing what we're doing now," he said.

She let out her breath. "And why it's so important to both of us to rescue women who can't or won't rescue themselves."

They were quiet for a moment, and she watched as he added the rest of the ingredients, making a thick sauce that smelled delicious.

Gradually the tension from their discussion evaporated and they eased into talking about work and what was going on at the station.

As he finished making dinner, she got out a couple of plates and silverware, and looked into the fridge for something to drink. "I have plenty of Heineken or water. I'm going for the beer—I can really use one."

"I'll take a beer, too." He glanced over his shoulder at her. "What about your pain meds?"

She drew out one bottle of beer at a time with her free hand and set them on the countertop. "Not taking anything but ibuprofen, and my last dose was four hours ago. I'm hoping the beer will do the trick now."

"I should have known." He put the pan of sauce on a cold burner and opened up both bottles of beer using an opener stuck to the side of the fridge with a magnet. She didn't argue that she could do it herself because her shoulder ached.

When they sat down to eat, Reese spooned tortellini and salad onto her plate. Again, the stubborn part of her thought about telling him she could do it herself but secretly she had to admit she liked him cooking for her and just being there. Why she liked it was a reason she didn't want to explore further than the fact that they'd been partners for some time now and she cared about him. A lot.

"You're more useful as a partner than I ever realized." She took a bite of the tortellini and gave a blissful sigh. "And a damned good cook."

He grinned. "Glad to be of some use."

She had just taken a bite of her salad when Reese said, "Something was bothering you earlier today."

The observation made her hesitate as she chewed. But then she finished and swallowed. "Why do you say that?"

"My keen investigative senses." He studied her. "And Nikki said you were really upset earlier but wouldn't talk about it."

Kelley pushed her food around her plate, not wanting to meet his eyes. "I'm over it now."

"You know you can talk to me," he said quietly.

She thought about telling him everything she'd told Johan. But a part of her was afraid of being perceived as weak in any way. She'd told him about her past, but telling him about how she'd lost it earlier today went too far. Reese was her partner, damn it. Not to mention she didn't want to go back and dredge up more about her family.

"It was nothing." She bit into a piece of garlic toast that had been made with fresh garlic and butter. When she finished chewing she said, "This is great." She looked at him and smiled. "This whole dinner is fantastic."

He looked at her, obviously knowing that she was doing her best to change the subject. He seemed to accept the fact that she wasn't going to talk about what she'd been upset about earlier. If she was honest with herself, she was still upset, but she wasn't going to let her grandmother dictate her mood.

"How is the search going for Taynor and that other bastard?" She sobered as she asked the question. "Any good leads?"

"Nothing that has led anywhere." Reese eyed her squarely. "Don't worry, Kelley. We'll find them."

She pushed her fingers through her hair. "Do you have any idea of how hard it is to sit on the sidelines when you need to be out there finding the bastards who kidnapped a little girl?"

"Yeah, I do." He nodded. "It sure as hell isn't easy. Especially when it hits close to home."

"That's putting it mildly," she said in a grumble.

He managed to guide their conversation elsewhere and she let him. Right this minute there wasn't anything she could do, but try and enjoy the evening. The beer helped her to relax, too.

The chocolate cake they had after dinner was so good it, along with Reese's company, greatly improved her mood. After she managed to keep herself from licking her plate clean of chocolate Ganache, they cleared the table and loaded the dishwasher.

When they were finished, he said, "I'd better get going."

She found herself inexplicably disappointed that he was leaving and she wished he could stay a little longer. Maybe she could ask him if he wanted to watch a movie?

But all she said was, "Thank you for dinner and dessert."

"Any time," he said as they walked to the front door.

He turned to face her and their gazes met and held. She felt like she couldn't breathe and she couldn't look away from his blue eyes. She thought she might melt from the heat of his gaze.

For the first time since they'd become partners, she wanted him to kiss her, wanted to taste him. She wanted his touch more than anything in this world, to feel his callused fingers brushing her skin. She wanted to nuzzle his neck and inhale his familiar scent and fill her lungs with it.

She swallowed as she held herself back from throwing herself into his arms. "Good night, Reese." Her words came out low and throaty.

He gave a nod. "Good night, Kelley."

And then he opened the door and walked into the night.

Reese blew out his breath as he walked down the steps to his truck. He unlocked it with the remote but the lights didn't flash or the alarm beep since there were times when he had to go out on a call when he was in the truck instead of the car he normally used for work.

Damn, he must be losing his marbles. When he'd reached for the doorknob and had looked into Kelley's eyes, he'd wanted to take her into his arms and kiss her with everything he had. He wanted to more than kiss her. He'd wanted to take her to bed.

He ground his teeth. That was no way to be thinking about his partner. They had a solid working relationship and had for some time now. The last thing he needed to do was try to kiss her and ruin that relationship.

Before the insanity of wanting to kiss her, most of the night his thoughts had stayed on Kelley's past. He'd already known at least part of her story, but hadn't wanted to tell her that he had researched it. She probably wouldn't have liked that he'd taken that upon himself. No doubt she'd want to kick his ass.

With his jaw set, he headed back to his ranch that wasn't too far from town. It wasn't really much of a ranch, but it was what he called home. He had a horse, a couple of steers that he raised for beef, and a mutt named Ruff.

When he reached home, Ruff bounded out to meet him in the driveway. Reese killed the engine and climbed out of the truck, and Ruff greeted him with enthusiasm. The dog was definitely man's best friend and Reese gave him an affectionate rub behind the ears.

Reese locked up his truck and headed into the house with Ruff at his side. Ruff had one ear that perked up and the other flopped down, and he almost always had a doggy smile. Reese had taken him in as a stray, and guessed the dog was part Australian shepherd, part Lab, and part Dalmatian. It was hard to tell due to Ruff's crazy quilt of brown and black spots on white, and he had one green eye and the other was blue.

Ruff happily trotted at Reese's side as he walked and sat as Reese unlocked the door. The dog waited for permission to go in and Reese gave him the sign to come inside the house.

Reese couldn't get Kelley and what had happened tonight off his mind. Maybe it was the fact that she'd come so close to death— twice now—that made him feel more protective toward her, and like he might have feelings for her beyond their partnership.

The living room was what his mom called rustic. He wasn't into decorating, so she'd taken it upon herself to do it for him, and he had to admit she'd done a good job. The house suited him with the overstuffed brown leather and wood couches, the coffee table on a tree trunk with end tables that looked like they were sitting on wagon wheels. Native American and western artwork was on the walls and a brown and a white cowhide rug was on the floor.

A large-screen TV was in the entertainment center where he liked to watch football and baseball games and the occasional movie.

He went to the kitchen and grabbed a can of beer out of the fridge before cracking it open and taking a long pull from it. He set the beer on the counter and grabbed a box of dog treats from the cabinet. He tossed one of the treats to Ruff who easily caught it before wolfing it down. Reese grabbed a large rawhide bone and gave it to the dog that happily took it and curled up on the dog bed beside the refrigerator to chew on it.

Reese thought about the similarities between his and Kelley's backgrounds. The big difference was the fact that he could pick up the phone and call his mom, and that was something Kelley would never be able to do.

While he drank his beer and watched Ruff chew on the rawhide, Reese leaned back against the counter. Guilt pressed down on his chest. He didn't call or see his mom nearly enough—his work took up so much of his days. Hell, he'd just have to make a point of visiting her and his stepdad more often. He loved his stepdad like a real dad and could care less about his bio-father.

Reese thought about Kelley again. He'd really like to introduce her to his mother. No doubt in his mind that they would like each other.

He pushed away from the counter and took a last drink of his beer before heading to his bedroom, hoping for a good night's sleep despite the fact he couldn't get Kelley off his mind.

CHAPTER 5

The morning after he'd made dinner at Kelley's place, Reese parked his car in front of Dickey's Auto Shop, following up on a lead in the Taynor case that he'd been given by the owner of the Highlander Bar. Reese couldn't help but think how much he missed having Kelley with him—they made a great team.

After he climbed out of the car, he headed into the auto shop. It was a hot summer's day but the breeze helped to cool things down.

When he entered one of the two bays, he saw a pair of overall-covered legs sticking out from under a truck on the left and an office to the right.

"Bill Dickey?" Reese called out.

"Hold on," came a muffled voice from beneath the truck.

Reese heard a clank and then a moment later a man rolled out from beneath the truck. The wiry man got to his feet and started wiping grease off his fingers with a blackened rag he'd pulled out of his back pocket. His fingernails and hands were black from working on vehicles.

"I'm Bill," the man said. "What do you need?"

"I'm Detective McBride with the Prescott Police Department." Reese pulled aside his overshirt as he showed the man the gold badge attached to his belt.

Looking wary, Bill stuffed the dirty rag into his back pocket. "What can I help you with?"

"Do you know this man?" Reese held out a picture and watched Bill as he looked at it.

Bill hesitated then gave a nod. "That's Darrell Taynor."

"How do you know Darrell?" Reese asked.

"I play cards with the boys every now and then in the back room at the Highlander. When Darrell has some kind of big payday, he'll join in." Bill chuckled. "Idiot will lose every damned dime he has and still he comes back for more, always thinking the next time will be his lucky day."

Reese studied Bill. "What kind of payday?"

Bill shrugged. "Always wanted to know but never asked." He looked like he was thinking hard about something and Reese waited for him to speak. "Stan was in the business with Darrell, whatever it was. Stan was the one who got Darrell in on the games. Stan's not much better a card player than Darrell is."

"What's Stan's last name?" Reese was good at keeping his expression neutral. "Where can I find him?"

"Don't know his last name." Bill frowned as he thought about Reese's questions. "But I do know he works part-time at that new sports center on the other side of town."

Reese handed Bill a business card. "If you see Darrell or Stan, give me a call."

"Sure." Bill took the card and slipped it into the breast pocket of his coveralls. "I'll do that."

As Reese walked away from the auto shop, he glanced over his shoulder and saw that Bill had turned his back and was talking on a cell phone. Reese reached his car and climbed in, wondering exactly who Bill had just called.

After Reese reached his car and climbed in, he drove to the opposite side of town to the new sports center. The old batting cages that had been part of an arcade and a hot dog stand weren't around anymore. The old cages had been there since Reese was a kid, which had been a good long time ago. He'd been there many times in his youth when it had been a local hangout.

When he reached the entrance to the sports center, he went into the air-conditioned building. It had five indoor batting cages along with a bungee trampoline, a sports simulator, and a concession stand as well as outdoor batting cages. The center had only been around a year and during the summer while the kids were out of school, it was even busier than it was during the rest of the year. The air conditioning had a hand in that.

Reese knew the owner of the sports complex, Noah Johnson. At the front entrance, Reese saw Noah's teenage daughter, Wendy.

"Hi, Detective McBride." The young woman had a pretty smile, red hair, as well as freckles over the bridge of her nose. "Dad's not here today."

"Hi, Wendy." Reese returned her smile. "Do you have someone named Stan working here?"

"He called in sick again today." She frowned. "He's been missing a lot of work lately, so between you and me I don't know if Dad's going to keep him around much longer."

Reese pulled his notebook and pen out of his pocket. "What's Stan's last name?"

"Driscoll." She looked at her computer screen. "We have his picture on file and I can give you his address if you want it."

"Perfect." Reese flipped open the notebook as she angled her screen so that he could see it. He glanced at the photo and noted the pimply face, Adam's apple, and shaggy reddish-brown hair. He jotted down the address that he recognized as being in a trailer park on the south side of town.

Wendy glanced at the door where a couple of teenage boys were coming into the building.

Reese gave her a smile when she looked back at him. "Thanks, Wendy."

"Bye, Detective." She smiled again and he left and headed out the entrance.

He walked back to his car, his gut telling him to call John. The name Stan Driscoll sounded familiar.

"What's up?" John answered on the second ring.

Reese climbed into his vehicle. "Tell me who Stan Driscoll is."

"We've had our eye on him," John said. "We just got information that leads us to believe he's gotten himself involved with local drug trafficking."

Reese jammed his keys into the ignition and started the car. "He might know where Darrell Taynor is. Petrova's still out. Would you like to join me in paying Driscoll a visit?"

"You bet." John took down the address as Reese read it off to him. "I'll meet you there," John said before disconnecting the call.

Fifteen minutes later, Reese reached the trailer park, found the space number, and parked on the private street, across from the mobile home. He got out of his car and leaned up against it as he waited for John. The mobile home was in poor repair with faded metal siding and weeds sprouting around the yard. A beat-up rusted white Toyota Corolla was parked in the carport. The other homes in the vicinity seemed to be in better condition. Stan's place looked to be the sore thumb of the neighborhood.

John pulled up in his police cruiser and parked behind Reese's car. John was in uniform and when he joined Reese, they both started for the front door. Just as they reached the foot of the driveway, the door opened and a tall, skinny, pimply-faced young man stepped out of the door and closed it behind him. It was the same guy as in the photograph that Wendy had showed him at the sports complex, Stan Driscoll.

Stan turned, saw Reese and John, and froze. He gave them one terrified look and ran.

"Oh, hell no," Reese muttered as he and John took off after the kid.

John went to the right and Reese to the left as they chased Stan around the mobile homes and through the trailer park. Stan dodged in and around lots and headed for a tall chain link fence that surrounded the trailer park.

Reese slid across the hood of a Nissan, cutting the distance between him and Stan.

Stan started climbing up the chain link fence. Reese reached the fence and grabbed one of Stan's legs. The man was halfway over the fence but Reese jerked him backward. John grabbed Stan's other leg and together he and Reese pulled Stan to the ground.

For a moment Stan fought to get away but then the fight left him and he went limp as John cuffed him and dragged him to his feet.

"I didn't do it." Stan's pimply face was dirty from having landed on the ground face first at the foot of the fence. "I didn't do nothing."

"Well that's odd." Reese put his hand on Stan's shoulder. "Seeing that you just ran and resisted arrest. Now why would you do that if you didn't do anything?"

Stan looked down at his feet as John grabbed his upper arm and marched him to the cruiser. John pushed Stan up against the cruiser and emptied his pockets.

"This'll get you some time." John pulled a baggie of a white crystalline substance out of Stan's pocket.

"It's not mine." Stan looked panicked. "It's a friend's."

"We'll have a talk downtown." Reese slapped Stan on the shoulder. "You're under arrest for possession of an illegal narcotic and for resisting arrest."

Stan hung his head as John read him his rights and pushed him into the back seat of the cruiser.

Down at the station, Stan had been put into an interrogation room to be questioned. He was handcuffed to the table and didn't bother looking up when Reese entered the room.

Reese glanced at the one-way mirror then took a chair and sat in it across from Stan. "Look at me," Reese said.

Stan looked up from under lank hair. "I didn't do nothing."

"Let's start over." Reese gave Stan a hard look. "You've already been busted for possession. Now we talk about murder, kidnapping, and shooting a cop."

"All I did was a little coke." Stan's eyes widened. "I didn't kill or kidnap or shoot no one. I don't even have a gun."

"How well do you know Darrell Taynor?" Reese asked.

Stan had a deer in the headlights look. "Don't know him."

Reese blew out his breath. "We already know that you play cards with him and the boys at the Highlander when you're flush. So why don't you start telling the truth. Like where you've been helping him hide that little girl."

"I don't know anything about a kid." Stan licked his lips, looking even more scared than before. "I should get a lawyer."

"You're better off telling me how you know Taynor and where he is now." Reese gave Stan a hard look. "I'd like to know what we'll find when we get a warrant to search your place."

"Nothing." The man started shaking and his eyes darted from Reese to the one-way glass and back to Reese. "Listen, I'll tell you what I know, but you gotta cut me a deal."

"First we'll see what information you can give me." Reese leaned forward, resting one arm on the table. "Start talking. Now."

"Darrell and me—we've done a little business." Stan licked his lips again. "I don't know if he's there now, but he has this place he likes to hang out at."

"Where?" Reese's body tensed.

Stan was bouncing all over the place. "It's where Darrell stashes the drugs when the shipments come in from down by the border." Stan rattled off an address not far from the trailer park Stan lived in. Reese knew Prescott like the back of his hand and knew exactly where the neighborhood was that Stan was talking about. "Is that enough to get me a deal?" Stan asked with a hopeful note in his voice.

"Not even close." Reese got to his feet. "Be thinking on what else you're going to tell me when I get back. And it had better be everything."

Stan slumped down in his seat, looking resigned.

Reese left the interrogation room and shut the door behind him. Stan had broken easier than Reese would have expected.

Everything was being set into motion even as he came out. John had been watching through the one-way glass and was already mobilizing the police officers to go to the address where Taynor could be hiding out with Belle.

"Let's go," Reese said and headed out the door.

Reese and his team set up down the street from the address Stan had given up. Reese and the rest of the raid team strapped on bulletproof vests and prepared to go in.

When they were ready, Reese led the way. The team surrounded the place and Reese went up the stairs of the small, rundown house.

He stood at the door, knocked, and called out, "Police. We're coming in."

No answer. Reese nodded to the officers with the battering ram. With a crash they opened the door, almost taking it off its hinges. Reese and his team entered the house, searching and clearing each room.

Reese's heart rate picked up as they searched the house and he prayed they'd find Belle here and that she would be alive and well.

The house was empty. Reese ground his teeth as he stood in the kitchen and pushed his fingers through his hair. He'd hoped like hell that they would find Taynor and Belle.

"Reese." John's voice came from Reese's left and he turned to see John holding up a dirty pink sock in his gloved hand. "Found this."

Reese narrowed his gaze as he looked at the sock. He recognized it as looking like one of the socks that the girl had been wearing the day Taynor abducted her. Reese took an evidence bag out of his pocket, held it open, and John dropped the sock into the bag.

"Find anything else?" Reese asked.

John shook his head. "No, but I'll keep looking."

Reese and the team searched the place, including checking the attic. In the attic they found close to a hundred thousand dollars worth of crack cocaine. All over the house they discovered stashes of cash—in shoeboxes in the closet, under a floorboard, in the kitchen in an empty cracker box, and taped to the backs of picture frames.

"Almost two hundred grand," John said as officers finished stacking the bills in the center of the living room.

"If Taynor was here, he must have left in a hurry." Reese frowned. "I'd doubt he'd leave all of this cash otherwise." Reese pushed his fingers through his hair again in a frustrated movement. "Who could have warned Taynor that we were coming?" Reese asked his stepbrother.

"Stan Driscoll never had a chance to." John shook his head. "Unless Taynor and he had worked something out. Maybe if Driscoll never showed up then Taynor would know he had to leave."

"Maybe." Reese considered it, then remembered Bill Dickey talking on his phone as Reese left the auto shop. "Or he was warned by a friend of his I met with earlier."

"Someone else to bring down to the station?" John asked.

Reese gave a slow nod. "I think it might be a good idea to bring in Bill Dickey."

"The owner of Dickey's Auto Shop?" John asked. "I'll pick him up."

"That's the one." Reese headed toward the front door and John fell into step beside him. "I'll head on over, too," Reese said.

"I don't know where Darrell Taynor and his kid are." Bill Dickey sat behind the table in the interrogation room, his hands gripped into fists on the tabletop. "I told you I barely know the guy."

"You're up to your neck in Taynor's and Driscoll's side business." Reese leaned up against the corner of the table. "How long have you been dealing dope?"

"I don't deal dope." Something flickered in Dickey's eyes, telling Reese the man wasn't being honest about something. "I don't know what they've gotten themselves into, but I don't care what it is and I don't have anything to do with it."

Reese studied Dickey. "Who did you call when I left this morning? I saw you on the phone."

Dickey looked surprised then uncomfortable. "I was talking with my woman."

"Is that your wife or girlfriend?" Reese asked.

"Girlfriend," Dickey muttered.

Reese's jaw tightened. "So you wouldn't mind if we check phone records to back that up?"

A droplet of sweat rolled down the side of Dickey's face. "You'd have to get some kind of warrant and you have nothing on me."

"We're talking about a little girl's life. You'd be surprised at how fast we can get a warrant." Reese pinned Dickey with his gaze. "Did you call Darrell Taynor and warn him we were looking for him?"

More sweat slid from Dickey's hair and down his temple. "No, damn it. I didn't call him."

Reese watched Dickey squirm. "Maybe it was because you didn't want us to find the drugs and cash."

Dickey shook his head. "No idea what you're talking about."

Reese continued to question Dickey, but the man wouldn't admit to a damned thing. Frustrated, Reese clenched his jaw. He knew Dickey was hiding something.

"You'll go to prison for aiding and abetting if you don't come clean," Reese said. "Think about that."

Dickey was looking more nervous by the moment, but he stuck to his story. "You can't keep me. I didn't do anything."

"We can keep you here for twenty-four hours." Reese started toward the door leading from the interrogation room. He paused and looked back at Dickey. "That will give you some time to think."

The man set his jaw and remained mute. Reese held back a growl of frustration and left the room.

John was waiting for him in the room on the other side of the one-way glass. "He's lying," John said.

Reese gave a nod. "He knows something. I don't know if it's related to the girl or to the drugs, but something's going on. I'm going to figure out exactly what that is."

Chapter 6

Jill Petrova screamed, the sound ripping through the night.

Heart thundering, Kelley ran into the house she'd grown up in, toward the sound of her mother's cry. Kelley bolted down the hallway leading to her parents' bedroom. She clenched her Glock in a tight grip as she raced down the hall as fast as she could.

The hallway seemed to grow longer as she ran. Her chest ached and her lungs burned from running so long, so fast. She pushed herself harder as she ran farther and farther.

Jill let out another blood-curdling scream that nearly made Kelley's heart stop.

Adrenaline pumped through Kelley's body. This time she would kill her father before he murdered her mother.

Just when she thought she'd never get there, Kelley reached the end of the hallway. She raced around the corner, into her parents' bedroom, and came to a full stop.

Ice chilled her veins and her mind spun.

Darrell Taynor, not Isaac Petrova, had his gun to Jill's head.

"Don't hurt my mother," Kelley tried to shout but she was mute, as if her mouth was covered by duct tape, and she couldn't get out the words.

"I'm going to kill her, Detective." Darrell sneered at Kelley, a look of satisfaction on his face. "There's nothing you can do about it."

Both anger and fear rose inside Kelley. Fear for her mother… Anger that Darrell had his gun to her head and was going to kill her.

Kelley's hands shook as she trained her weapon on Darrell.

From out of nowhere, ropes snaked around her like possessed vines, pulling her arms behind her back and tying her wrists. Her weapon fell to the floor and hit it with a hard thunk. The ropes squeezed her from her upper arms to her waist, and she almost blacked out from the pain of the rope crushing her wounded shoulder.

Kelley struggled to get free but the bonds were too tight. Fear for her mother magnified inside her and spun in a vortex of anger. She wanted to kill Darrell and save her mother.

She tried again to shout but now she was gagged, the rope holding cloth inside her mouth.

As she fought to get free to save her mother, Isaac Petrova eased from out of the shadows. Kelley stared in horror at the two men. Isaac stepped toward Kelley and he gripped the end of a belt. The buckle thumped on the floor as he dragged it closer to her.

He was going to whip her with the buckle like he had so many times before.

Kelley screamed and struggled, her gaze darting from Darrell to her mother to her father.

"No!" Her scream came out muffled by the gag as she tried to beg Darrell. She didn't care that Isaac was going to beat her. She just needed to save her mother.

Isaac raised the belt and swung it at Kelley. Stars burst in her mind as the buckle struck her head and her knees went weak. He swung the belt at her again, the buckle striking her cheek. She felt the skin break open and blood poured down her face from the gash.

No matter the pain, she stared at Darrell instead of her father. She tried to beg him with her eyes.

With a smile of pure evil, Darrell watched Kelley as he pulled the trigger.

Kelley screamed behind her gag again as the sound ricocheted around the room.

But it was Laura Jones, not Jill Petrova, who collapsed to the floor. A hole gaped in Laura's temple, a single drop of blood rolling out onto her white skin.

"Mommy!" Belle ran into the bedroom as she shrieked the word.

Kelley's gag was suddenly gone and she too cried out, "Mommy!"

Isaac's head swung as he turned his attention from Kelley to Jill who now appeared on her knees in front of him.

He dropped the belt and an iron fire poker was now in his hand.

Darrell's laugh echoed in the background.

Isaac brought the iron poker down—

Kelley woke up with a scream, sitting bolt upright in her dark bedroom as she fought against her sheets that were twisted around her like heavy ropes.

Heart thundering, she breathed in harsh gasps as she came to her senses. It was just a dream… Only a dream… Except that Jill and Laura really were dead.

Kelley's stomach felt sick as she touched her chin where Isaac had split the skin with the belt buckle. But there was only the pale thin scar left over from that day. The last day he'd ever beaten her because she'd fled that same night.

And he'd murdered her mother the very next morning.

A tear rolled down Kelley's cheek, over the fingers that still touched the scar. She could almost feel the burning pain from when the belt buckle had sliced her skin. But it meant nothing. She'd give any amount of pain, any amount of scars, to have her mother back.

With a deep, shuddering breath, she moved her fingers away from her cheek. When she glanced at the clock she saw that it was just after two a.m. She pushed away the tangled sheets and slid back down into bed, beneath her bedspread. She lay on her side, her head resting on her pillow.

She didn't want to sleep… Didn't want to see her mother's and Laura's dead faces again. For hours, she lay awake and stared into the darkness, trying to banish the images of Laura being murdered and Isaac starting to swing the iron poker at her mother's head.

Still in her nightgown, Kelley walked down the hall from the kitchen where she'd just nibbled on some toast for breakfast while drinking down a big mug of coffee. She passed her home office as she headed to her bedroom where she was going to change into the clothes she planned on wearing today.

She was so tired…she hadn't been able to sleep since the night Laura was murdered. Like last night, every other night she'd also been having nightmares. Her father and Darrell Taynor went in and out of her dreams, her mother's and Laura's dead faces burned into her mind.

The guilt that weighed so heavily on her would likely never go away and she'd have to live with it. Finding the man who had abducted Belle was something she had to do.

Her cell phone rang in her pocket and she pulled it out to see that it was Reese. Ever since her grandmother had stopped by, she'd been dreading hearing from the old woman again.

It was with some relief that she said, "What's up, Reese?"

"Checking in on my favorite partner," he said. "What are you up to?"

"I'm going to the shooting range in half an hour." Kelley paused in the middle of her bedroom. "The doc let me out of my sling yesterday and I want to get some practice in with my left hand."

"Damn it, Petrova." He sounded irritated. "You need to be resting your shoulder."

"Just try and stop me." Her tone was probably a little waspish, but she didn't care. She hated this feeling of being coddled. "Tell me about the Taynor case."

He ignored her request. "How are you getting to the range?"

She frowned. "Nikki is going to drop me off and then she'll pick me up when I'm finished."

"Call her and tell her I'm taking you." Reese said the words like it was an order. "It's my day off, and I need to get some time in on the range. I'll see you in thirty."

Kelley opened her mouth to tell him that she didn't need him watching over her, which was exactly what he was doing, but he'd disconnected the call. She held her phone out and glared at it. Grudgingly, she called Nikki and told her she didn't need a ride after all. Nikki made a crack about hot detective partners and Kelley almost hung up on her. But there was no arguing that she was right—Reese was damned hot.

As she got ready to go, she let her hair fall loosely because her shoulder still hurt too much to pull her hair into a ponytail. She dressed in a white scoop-necked T-shirt, her favorite soft and comfortable faded jeans, socks, and sturdy leather shoes. She stuffed her wallet with her credentials, cash, and credit cards in one pocket, shoved her keys in another, and then put on small silver earrings.

When she was dressed, she slid on a belt and a holster with her Glock. Trying not to jar her shoulder, she carefully shrugged into a sapphire blue blouse to cover her service weapon. She walked past her treadmill that she kept in her bedroom. It was frustrating not to be able to go jogging in the mornings. The treadmill just wasn't the same, but she was still using it to help keep in shape.

The doorbell rang and she headed from her bedroom to the living room. She opened the front door to see Reese on her doorstep. A flutter went through her belly for the first time ever with him. It was different from the warm, squishy feeling in her belly she'd gotten when he'd cooked dinner for her. Even compared to how sexy he was the other night, she never remembered him looking so good as he did right now. He wore a black Stetson, an open western shirt over a black T-shirt, Wrangler jeans, and black boots. He had a day's growth of stubble and his blue eyes were studying her in a way that made her feel like he was seeing her in the same way—as something more than just a partner.

But then it could have been her imagination or wishful thinking. Treading those waters was dangerous, something she had to keep reminding herself.

"Ready?" He gave her a smile that made her insides do funny things that they shouldn't be doing.

"Yes." She nodded as she patted her holstered Glock. "Let's get to the range. I can't wait to shoot something."

He gave her a grin. "That's the partner I know and love."

Even though she wasn't wearing a sling now, she still needed to baby her shoulder, so she let him help her up into the truck.

As he drove to the shooting range, she drilled him about the Taynor case. "Has the case progressed at all?" When he frowned at her question, she knew it had. "There's something you've found," she stated.

Reese gave a slow nod. "All of the leads have ended up in dead ends until yesterday." He hesitated as Kelley sat straighter in her seat. "We're pretty sure that Taynor has ties to a drug cartel in southern Arizona."

Her eyes widened. "And you didn't tell me?"

"I wasn't certain until today." Reese explained what had gone down with Bill Dickey and Stan Driscoll yesterday. "It wasn't until this morning that Dickey finally caved in and gave us what we needed to know about Taynor and the drug smuggling ring he's involved with."

"I want in on this, Reese," she said and could hear the stubbornness in her own voice. "For all we know, since he has ties to a cartel, he could be across the line with that little girl."

"It's possible." By Reese's expression, she could tell that he was as frustrated as she was. "But we had a damned good lead from a snitch that he was still here locally," Reese said. "Taynor must have left not long before we got to the house where he was stashing drugs and cash. So as far as we know, he's still in Prescott. Our snitch told us there's something in the works, which is the only reason why Taynor hasn't left town yet."

She shook her head. "How has he eluded us for so long?"

Reese glanced from the road to her. "I think there's a good chance he was prepared for something to go down and found a place to hide out until things cool off. He may have planned on kidnapping Belle all along."

"Damn him," Kelley said through gritted teeth.

She frowned. "I can't believe I didn't think of it earlier, but something important just occurred to me."

"It could have been the concussion that made you forget," he said. "So what did you remember?"

"During a conversation I had with Laura, she mentioned a foster brother." Kelley frowned. Usually she recalled conversations easily, but this one wasn't coming to her as clearly as normal. "This foster brother was bad news and he'd scared her when he'd come around."

Reese's brow furrowed. "When we checked out Taynor's background we saw that he'd been in the foster care system in Phoenix, but nothing came up about a foster brother who Taynor had been heavily involved with."

Kelley tilted her head to the side. "At the time, Laura hadn't wanted to go to the police and file a report because she was not only scared of Taynor but of his foster brother, too." Kelley pushed strands of hair behind her ear. "She was afraid that either one of them would kill her if they were arrested and let go for any reason."

"Do you remember the foster brother's name?" Reese asked.

For a moment Kelley thought about it. Her jaw ached from clenching it so tightly as she mentally dug for the information. "I've never had a problem with my memory." She wanted to scream in frustration. It seemed that the more she tried to think of it, the more her brain caused it to elude her.

"Hey." Reese glanced at her. "Concussions can take some time to heal. Be patient with yourself."

She shook her head, still thinking about the conversation with Laura. The name finally came to Kelley and she blew out her breath. "Johnny Rocha." She gave a mirthless laugh. "His friends called him Johnny Rocket, but she wasn't sure why."

"Probably has something to do with drugs," Reese said, looking thoughtful.

She nodded. "I think the next step is to track down Taynor's foster brother."

"I'll get hold of John and see if he can start in on it." Reese pulled his phone out of his holster and pressed a speed dial number before holding the phone to his ear.

Kelley listened as he spoke with John but wasn't sure what John said when Reese spoke with him.

When Reese ended the call and stuffed his phone into its holster, he said, "John isn't on duty but he said he'd get on the lead as soon as he gets in."

Kelley pushed her hair behind her one of her ears and looked out the window. She wondered if her concussion had anything to do with her having a hard time sleeping as well as having affected her memory.

She turned back to Reese. "Why don't we see what we can find out now?"

"Don't worry." Reese looked at the road then his eyes met hers. "We're going to find Taynor and Belle."

She just nodded. Finding the little girl was something Kelley intended to do, even if she hadn't been cleared to go back to work. She'd had enough of sitting on the sidelines.

Twenty minutes later, Kelley had earmuffs on, her Glock unholstered, standing at the firing point in the indoor shooting range. Reese stood behind her with his own earmuffs on, watching her. She squared off, aiming at the target, using her left hand. Because her right shoulder hurt so much, she was having a hard time with a two-handed grip, but she was determined.

The first target she imagined was her father. She did fairly well, but not acceptable as far as she was concerned—maybe it was the fact that no matter how much she hated her father, and how much he deserved it, she wouldn't shoot the bastard. She reeled it in and discarded the target before sending another one out.

Still using her left hand she pictured Taynor as the second target. Her anger magnified when she thought of him, her focus sharpening. When she finished, she pressed the button to bring the target toward her and took off her earmuffs. She tried not to grimace from the pain in her shoulder. It might not have been the smartest idea to come to the range today, but she didn't want to admit it.

Reese took off his earmuffs too, and shook his head when the target reached them. Her shots were grouped so close around the heart that the bullets had left one big hole.

"Damn, Petrova." Reese took down the target. "I knew you're a great shot with your right. Never knew you could shoot so well left-handed."

Kelley put a new clip in her Glock as she looked at Reese. "I was at the top in my class in the academy."

"Can't say that I'm surprised." Reese nodded to her gun. "If you had something lighter, it might hurt your shoulder less."

She shrugged then winced because of the pain it caused. "I'd like to get one of the newer lighter Glocks. Maybe down the road."

Reese sent a fresh target out and drew his Glock from his shoulder holster. He put his earmuffs back on and squared off with the target.

Kelley holstered her Glock and covered her ears with the muffs again. She watched as Reese took his turn. When he was finished and reeled the target back in, she studied the target and said, "Not bad."

He looked at the grouping that wasn't quite as tight as Kelley's. "Yeah, but you kicked my butt today. *And* you did it with an injury."

They continued practicing but Kelley had to call it quits after her third round. "I think I may have slightly overdone it."

He didn't give her a hard time like she'd expected. Instead, he put his hand on her good shoulder. "How about a big, greasy burger?"

She grinned. "And an ice-cold beer."

"The Highlander it is," he said.

CHAPTER 7

As he drove, Reese frowned to himself as he saw Kelley grimace when she thought he wasn't looking. Maybe overdoing it today would teach her not to be so stubborn in the future. He mentally shook his head. As if that was going to happen.

He parked in front of the Highlander Bar when they reached it. He knew better than to open car doors for her, but with her injury he figured that was an exception. She already had the truck door open when he went around to the passenger side. Considering how high his truck was and the fact that she was petite, she needed his help now.

When they walked into the bar, Reese squinted in the dimness. It was the middle of the afternoon so the place wasn't as busy as it would be in a couple of hours. Reese nodded to a couple of guys he knew before he and Kelley took a high top. After they were seated at the table, Sophie, a waitress with a short skirt and a low-cut blouse, took their order for two cheeseburgers with everything on them, as well as home fries and two Heinekens.

As the waitress walked away, Reese turned to look at Kelley. He'd always thought his partner was pretty, but it was as if he was seeing her in a new light. She was beautiful with her blonde hair loose around her face, her blue eyes so thoughtful looking, and her gentle curves. He wanted to touch those curves, to run his fingers through her silky hair and to kiss her soft lips.

"What's wrong?" She looked at him with her head tilted to the side.

He shook his head. "How's your shoulder?"

"A bit sore," Kelley admitted. Her face seemed a little pale and strained, but she still looked damned beautiful.

He knew better than to say anything like, "I told you so." Instead, he just nodded. "Give it a week or so and you'll be doing a lot better."

She frowned. "Patience has never been my strong suit."

"I noticed." He couldn't help a little smile.

She looked around. "Like why isn't my cheeseburger here already?"

He laughed. "Because you just ordered, honey."

They both froze and looked at each other. He didn't know whether to apologize for calling his partner "honey" or to just let it ride.

"Saved by the beer," he muttered as Sophie arrived with their bottles of Heineken.

Kelley laughed. She had such a sexy laugh that it made his gut tighten.

Both bottles were already open and Reese took a long pull of his. He needed to get his head on straight when it came to Kelley, and he needed to do it now.

When Kelley set her beer bottle down, she gave him a thoughtful look. "It's our anniversary next weekend."

Reese raised an eyebrow. "Anniversary?"

"Don't tell me you're a man who forgets special dates." She wore a teasing smile.

For the life of him he didn't know what she was talking about. "Uh—"

"What happened to your deductive skills?" She shook her head. "It's a sad day when you forget our anniversary. We've been partners for two years this Sunday."

Reese blew out his breath. Of course. "I didn't forget. I've just had my mind on the Taynor case."

She rolled her eyes. "Uh-huh."

"We'll go out to celebrate." He gave her a quick grin. He knew where her heart was. "Your shoulder should be better by then."

With a laugh she said, "It's a date." Her eyes widened and she held up her hands. "Not a real date."

"Of course not," he said, amused.

She grinned. "Can't wait."

By the time they left the Highlander it was dark. When they reached Kelley's home, Reese went to the passenger side and helped her out of the truck. He found himself wanting to hold her hand but released it as soon as her feet were firmly on the ground.

"Come in for a beer," she said as he walked her up to the door.

Reason warred within him, telling him that he shouldn't. But something deep inside him didn't want the day to end. "Sounds good," he said, shoving reason straight out the door.

Once they were inside, Kelley pointed to the sofa. "Have a seat. I'll grab the beer and be right back."

He gave a nod and seated himself on the sofa. A few minutes later and she reappeared with two green bottles of Heineken. She handed a bottle to him then set hers on the coffee table. He watched with a raised brow as she slipped out of the blue shirt she'd worn over her white T-shirt and tossed the shirt over the back of a chair. She unholstered her Glock and put the weapon into a drawer in the entryway table.

When she was finished, she sat on the couch a couple of feet from him. She faced him with her knees bent and her legs tucked under her.

His gut tightened as he watched her. "How's your shoulder?"

"I had some ibuprofen with me and I took it earlier." She rested the elbow of her good arm on the back of the sofa and studied him. "Right now I feel pretty good."

A part of him knew that it was a real bad idea to be sitting so close to her the way he was feeling right now. He drank from his beer bottle but his eyes never left hers. She looked so damned beautiful with her hair a little tousled, her blue eyes darkening with what looked like desire. Her lips parted and he thought he saw a hitch in her breathing.

It didn't take his detective skills to know that she wanted him as much as he wanted her. It was like something possessed him, not giving a damn about the fact that she was his partner. He set his beer bottle on the coffee table, scooted closer to her and took her bottle from her hand. Her eyes widened as he set her beer next to his.

Their gazes held, as if they couldn't get enough of looking at each other. He reached out to her and slowly brought his hands to her face and cupped it gently.

He waited for her to pull away, to tell him no. Instead she placed her hands on his chest, her touch warming his skin through his shirt.

Inch by inch he lowered his face to hers.

Kelley's heart beat faster as Reese's lips neared hers. She found herself holding her breath, wondering if she should let him kiss her, if she dared.

Through his shirt, his chest was warm against her palms and she clenched the soft material in her fingers. A heartbeat passed and then his mouth claimed hers.

Neither of them held anything back. The kiss was fierce, hungry, intense. His lips were firm and he tasted of beer and his own masculine flavor. She'd always liked his scent whenever she caught a whiff of it, but now it filled her lungs and she breathed deeply, drinking her fill.

She slid her hands up his chest and linked her fingers behind his neck. His skin felt hot. She felt on fire.

Soft moans rose up within her and her belly quivered when he growled in response. He moved his hands from her face, sliding his fingers down her neck, skimming her shoulders, clearly being careful of her injury.

Right now she felt no pain. She only felt heat and desire and a need so great she couldn't have stopped herself if she wanted to.

She didn't want to. No, she needed this more than anything. She *needed* Reese.

He pulled her onto his lap, caging her with one arm as they kissed. She felt his erection beneath her bottom and she wiggled, rubbing herself against it. He groaned against her lips and she grew damp between her thighs.

She moved in his embrace and straddled him and wished their clothes were gone so that nothing would be between them. She imagined what it would be like to ride him now, to feel him inside her as he fucked her.

Fuck. The word was unbelievably erotic, bringing with it visions of him taking her in ways she could only imagine. She wanted to make it real. She didn't want to have to imagine any longer.

She clenched her fingers tighter in his T-shirt and she made soft, hungry sounds as they kissed. Her desire for him magnified when he gently bit her lower lip.

The kiss grew hungrier, almost frantic. She slid one palm down to his waistband and below, and shifted so that she could feel his hard cock beneath her hand. She moved both hands to his belt buckle and fumbled with it, trying to unfasten it. It came undone and she went for the button of his jeans.

He groaned as she reached into his jeans and her fingers found his cock. She felt the satin and steel of his erection and squeezed it. He moved his lips to the curve of her neck. He caught both of her wrists in one of his hands before he raised his head and looked down at her.

Her chest rose and fell with every harsh breath she took as she met his gaze. She didn't want to stop. She wanted him with everything she had.

He lowered his head and placed his forehead against hers and she closed her eyes. She could tell his breathing was as heavy as hers.

"We need to stop." He said the words gruffly, as if angry with someone.

She drew back and met his gaze. "What's wrong?"

"This." He looked away before meeting her gaze again. "You're my partner and you're injured. This should never have happened. I don't want to ruin what we have."

It felt as if cold water had been dashed over her. She jerked her wrists away from his hold and scooted back from him so that there was a good two feet between them now.

"You're right," she said, but felt a part of her grow cold as she said the words. "Maybe you should go."

He held her gaze for a long moment before he gave a nod and got to his feet. "I'll see you later."

She stood, too. "Call me about the Taynor case tomorrow."

He studied her for a long moment. "All right," he said, and she wondered if he meant it, if he really would call her about the case.

She walked him to the front door and opened it. He stepped onto the porch and gave her one last look. He started to turn and she shut the door, not wanting to watch him walk away.

CHAPTER 8

Kelley sat at her desk in her home office, trying to keep her mind off of last night and the kiss she'd shared with Reese. She was finding it virtually impossible.

It had been a mistake, one she regretted. They'd let the moment get away from them and she hoped it wouldn't hurt their working relationship. Damn. How could she have let that happen?

She pushed her fingers through her hair as she stared at her notes on her iPad. Was Johnny Rocha, aka Johnny Rocket, the Taynor's foster brother? Had he been the one who'd shot her?

The ache in her shoulder was more pronounced after having gone to the shooting range yesterday. She'd never admit that to Reese or anyone else, but right now it wasn't a problem. She wasn't doing anything more strenuous than searching via her contacts for the mystery shooter, Taynor, and Belle.

Kelley kept one informant in particular, Zip Moore, in her phone contacts because he somehow always knew what was going on when it came to anything illegal. He wouldn't talk with anyone on the force but her. She pressed his number on her phone.

He answered on the second ring. "Who is this?"

"I need to ask you a few questions about someone named Johnny Rocha," she said. No doubt he knew exactly who'd called when he'd heard her voice.

"Johnny Rocket?" Zip's voice grew hard as he said the name. "I'd be crazy to talk to you about him."

"It's important." She gripped her phone tighter. "Tell me what you know. I'll make it worth your while, like always."

A pause. "Not over the phone," Zip said after a moment. "I'll meet you at the usual place."

It would take ten minutes to get to the abandoned farm. She glanced at her watch. "Twenty minutes."

"Now? I don't think I can—"

She cut him off in a warning tone. "Zip, you know you're safe with me."

He blew out his breath. "All right, all right. Make sure you're not followed."

She disconnected the call, and with a smile of satisfaction went from her office to her bedroom and tugged on a pair of shoes. It felt good to be moving forward on this case.

Technically she wasn't cleared to drive yet, but she was tired of being cooped up and dependent on others. It wouldn't hurt to meet Zip on her own—he was as dangerous to her as a newborn kitten.

She shoved her wallet with her credentials in the back pocket of her jeans and her keys in her front pocket. She buckled on her belt and holstered her Glock, then put a light blazer on over her blouse to cover her weapon.

It took her all of eight minutes to get ready to go and then she was out the door and in her dark green Ford Explorer. As she drove to the meeting place, her heart beat a little faster from the thrill of the hunt. Every step she took would take her closer to Taynor and Belle.

Zip wasn't at the meeting place at the abandoned farm when she arrived. She drove around to the back side of a dilapidated weathered barn and parked. The farm was far enough off the main road that they most likely wouldn't be seen, but she never took chances if she could help it.

She parked her SUV in the shade and climbed out, then leaned against the vehicle and looked up at an old rusted windmill that creaked in the warm breeze. Her hair lifted from her shoulders and a dust devil skittered across barren land a hundred feet away from her. Two vultures circled overhead and she wondered if some poor creature had died and had the vultures' attention.

Zip arrived five minutes after she did, and he pulled up in his sapphire blue 1969 Camaro. It had a wide white stripe down the middle of the hood and she knew the car was his baby.

When he got out of the car, he pulled a cigarette out of a pack in his shirt pocket and a lighter from his jeans' front pocket. He paused to cup his hand against the breeze so that he could light the cigarette.

After it was lit, he slipped the lighter back into his pocket and walked toward her. His dirty blond hair reached his collar and he had a scar like a slash through one eyebrow. His skin was tanned and lined and he looked older than his thirty-five years.

"Hello, Detective." He drawled the words as he leaned against the hood of his Camaro. "Sure you want to get into Johnny Rocket's business?"

"What kind of question is that?" She scowled and pushed away from the Explorer, and walked up to him. He was thin and lanky, a good eight inches above her five-two. "I'll get in anyone's business who gets in my way. And if Johnny has anything to do with a little girl's disappearance you can be damned sure I'll serve up his balls to him on a platter."

Zip took a hit on his cigarette and blew out the smoke. "I'll say one thing. You've got your own set of brass balls, Detective." He shook his head. "Johnny is real bad news."

"Why haven't I heard of him before?" Kelley asked. "Prescott Valley isn't exactly a metropolis with new drug kingpins sprouting out of the desert."

"The man's a ghost." Zip blew out another puff of smoke. "And he's new around here—came up from Phoenix. You know the Hector Garcia murder, the one you cops haven't figured out yet?"

Kelley frowned. "You're telling me this Rocha guy is involved?"

Zip smirked. "Johnny's the one who offed him."

A chill rolled up her spine. Hector Garcia had been one of the most notorious drug smugglers around, and smart, too. For someone to have the opportunity to kill him, they had to have been just as smart. Reese and Kelley had been trying to make a case against Garcia when he'd turned up dead, just weeks ago. Someone had done the Prescott Police Department a big favor.

She and Reese had been investigating the murder but they'd both been injured on another case, which had slowed things way down. The workload of the other detectives on the force was heavy right now so the Garcia murder had been put on the sidelines. Kelley being shot, Belle's kidnapping, and Laura's murder, had taken precedence.

The breeze blew strands of hair across Kelley's eyes and she impatiently brushed them out of her face. "Tell me what you know about Rocha."

Zip shrugged. "He has a major shipment coming in soon that will make him a big player in the area. He's already got an established business in Phoenix. He's seeking to expand."

"I'm going to want details on that shipment." Her heart rate had picked up. "But first I want to know if Rocha has the girl, Belle Jones."

A scowl creased Zip's face. "I don't like no one messing with kids."

Something caught in Kelley's throat. "So he is involved."

Zip's scowl deepened. "The sonofabitch is into trafficking kids."

Her skin went cold and for a moment she felt lightheaded and wondered if it was the concussion. "Are you saying he sold Belle?"

"Don't know." Zip shook his head. "But he could have or he's gonna do it."

"Do you know where Rocha and Taynor are?" The words rushed out. Dear God, she had to find Belle.

Zip raked his fingers through his hair. "Last I heard, Rocha was at Fat T's place. Johnny's looking to set up shop somewhere and I think he's liking Fat T's."

"You're certain?" Kelley's jaw was tight. She knew exactly the location Zip was referring to.

The informant gave a nod. "I don't hold no love for any bastard who sells kids."

"Give me what you know about the drug shipment," she said even as she was pulling out her phone and pressing the speed dial number for Reese.

"I don't have that information yet, but I'll get it." Zip held out his hand. "In the meantime."

Kelley pulled out her wallet and gave the informant cash while at the same time holding her phone between her ear and shoulder.

Reese answered as she turned away from Zip and hurried back to her Explorer.

"Hi, Kelley," Reese said, and she swallowed. He usually said, "What's up, Petrova?" Apparently last night *had* changed things.

She climbed into her Explorer, the phone now in her hand. "I just met with Zip—"

"What?" Reese cut across what she was saying. "What the hell were you doing out meeting an informant? You should have called me and let me take care of it."

"Listen to me." Kelley nearly shouted as she started the vehicle. "This is important. It's about Belle."

"I'm listening," Reese said.

As she drove the SUV away from the old ranch, Kelley told Reese the entire conversation she'd just had with Zip.

Reese cursed. "I'll mobilize the team."

"I'll meet you there," she said and disconnected the call before he could tell her to stay home.

With her jaw set, she headed down the dirt road, back to the main road toward town, straight for Fat T's.

She beat Reese and his team by one minute. She parked her Explorer as law enforcement vehicles pulled up. After she cut the engine, she jumped out and opened up the back of her SUV where she took off her blazer and pulled on a bulletproof vest and then a windbreaker with POLICE across the back.

Reese strode up toward her, his expression fierce. "No. You're still on leave."

"I'm getting in on the raid." She scowled at him. "We don't have time to argue. Let's go."

For one moment they glared at each other and then Reese started giving out orders to the officers to cover the back and the front of Fat T's place.

Kelley went with Reese to the front door with officers backing them up. Two men swung the battering ram at the door. A huge crash sounded in the air as the door splintered open.

"Police!" Reese shouted, as did Kelley and the other officers as they swept into the home. Their shouts echoed in the house, organized chaos. Three men, including Fat T, were playing poker in the living room. Cards and poker chips went flying when the table overturned as the men rushed to their feet.

One of the men pulled a gun. Reese shot him and the man went down. Fat T and the other man put their hands behind their heads and dropped to their knees like they were told and then they were handcuffed and jerked to their feet.

Reese, Kelley, and the officers continued through the house, shouting "Police!"

Someone jarred Kelley's shoulder and the pain made her bite her cheek. She tasted blood but ignored it as they continued clearing the house.

They didn't find anyone else in the house and Kelley's heart sank. They did find crack cocaine stashed throughout the place, but that was no consolation as far as she was concerned.

Heat flushed through her body as she marched out the front door and straight up to Fat T who was being held by two officers as they walked toward a cruiser.

"Hold on," Kelley told the officers. To Fat T she shouted, "Where's the girl? Where's Belle?"

He smirked. "Ain't no girl 'round here."

"So help me," she said with narrowed eyes. "You will tell me or I'll kick your balls up into your throat and you can choke on them."

His throat worked as if he was trying to swallow something. "You wouldn't."

She poked his chest, her finger pushing into his fat. "Try me, you sonofabitch."

"They left." Sweat was on Fat T's brow and his wife-beater T-shirt had damp sweat rings under his armpits. "I don't know nothin' else."

Reese came up beside Kelley. "We'll take him down to the station and we'll get it out of him."

Kelley's hands clenched into fists at her sides. "They were just here. We need to track them down, now. If I have to make this bastard sing falsetto, then I will."

Reese looked at Fat T who was shaking his head. "Darrell and Johnny, they left with that little girl. I told you."

"When?" Kelley growled.

"Maybe half an hour ago." Fat T's dark little eyes darted from Kelley to Reese and back. "They didn't say where they were going. Johnny, he doesn't tell me anything."

"Right." She gave a nod to the officers who held Fat T. They pushed him into the back seat of the cruiser as one of the officers read Fat T his rights. He was so fat it was a wonder he fit into the vehicle and the car didn't drop like a low-rider from his weight.

Kelley raked her fingers through her hair. Her whole body ached with frustration. "We just missed them *again*." She looked up at Reese, who wore a grim expression. "What if he sells that little girl?" Terror at the thought of Belle being sold into child slavery made her whole body hurt.

"We're not going to let that happen." Reese rested one of his hands on her good shoulder. "We'll see what we can obtain from the other guy." He nodded toward another cruiser where the other man was sitting in the back. "Ron Simpson. He's just one of Fat T's flunkies, so I'm not sure what we'll get out of him."

A stabbing pain shot through Kelley's head and she wavered as her head spun a little. She hesitated, waiting out the dizzy spell.

"You all right?" Reese wore a concerned expression.

"I'm fine." She straightened.

John walked up to them, carrying what looked like a computer's hard drive. "Grabbed this." He raised it so that they could see it. "Might get lucky and find something on it."

"Good." Reese gave a nod and John turned away.

Kelley put her hands on her hips. "I'm going with you to the station."

Reese shook his head. "Captain Johnson is going to be pissed enough when he finds out you were here. Let me handle the interrogations and I'll tell you what we get out of them."

Another stab of pain had Kelley gritting her teeth. "You'll tell me everything," she demanded.

He gave a nod. "Everything." He glanced at her SUV. "I'm going to have someone drive you home"

"It's not far." She started taking off the windbreaker with POLICE across the back. "I'm fine."

Reese studied her for a long moment. "You need to take care of yourself, Petrova."

She might have smiled as he referred to her by her last name if her head hadn't hurt so badly. It suddenly felt like nothing had changed between them.

"I'll be waiting for your call," she said and turned away.

Reese watched Kelley go. Damn but he didn't want to let her drive home alone. His instincts had been to take her in his arms and hold her close to him. Of course he couldn't do that and undermine her.

With a curse beneath his breath, he clenched and unclenched his hands. If he kept worrying about her every time they went out into the field, he was going to get one of them killed. He had to keep his mind on the job.

He ground his teeth. He wasn't so sure he could work with Kelley as his partner much longer. He'd become far too overprotective of her. She was good at what she did and he'd seen her take down grown men over twice her size. But everything had changed with that kiss last night.

The kiss. For a moment he closed his eyes and shut out the sounds around him as he remembered her soft lips and sweet kiss, and how willing she'd been… If he hadn't put a stop to it, who knew what would have happened.

With a low growl, he opened his eyes and shook his head. Yeah, he knew exactly what would have happened, and he'd be regretting last night even more than he already was.

CHAPTER 9

To get his mind off of Kelley, Reese immersed himself in wrapping up the scene and then headed back to the station to interrogate Fat T and the other suspect. Despite his promise to her, he didn't want to tell Kelley what they might learn from the two they had in custody or if they found anything on the hard drive. She was likely to go tearing off on her own again if they had something substantial.

She was a damned good detective and it was thanks to her investigative skills and contacts that they'd come this close to finding Belle. They needed Kelley's keen mind, but it was more important that she recover and be at full speed when she returned.

All the way back to the station, Reese worked to pull himself together. That included putting his relationship with Kelley to the back of his mind.

When he reached the station, Reese went to the interrogation room that Fat T was being held in. Ron Simpson was in another.

Reese entered the investigation room where Fat T's wrists were zip tied to a bar on the table he was sitting behind—his wrists were too fat for regular handcuffs. He was so large he barely fit on the chair, his fat hanging over the edges of his seat. His stomach extended like a king-sized beach ball beneath a dirty white wife-beater T-shirt, pressing against the table and likely making it uncomfortable to be cuffed in that position.

Fat T wasn't much of a threat. He couldn't get out of his chair fast enough to begin with, so Reese cut the zip tie cuffs.

"Thanks," Fat T mumbled and rubbed his reddened fat wrists.

"You're facing prison time." Reese sat on a chair at the opposite side of the table. "That was one hell of a lot of crack cocaine we found in your house."

Fat T licked his lips. Even his tongue looked fat. "I can't go to prison." Reese could smell the stink of the man's sweat.

Reese held no sympathy for the scumbag. "Should have thought of that before you started dealing out of your house. Don't bother to say it's not yours."

Drops of sweat beaded on Fat T's forehead, his whole face and thick neck slick with perspiration. He stared at the table.

Reese leaned back in his chair. "Tell me about Johnny Rocket."

Eyes wide, Fat T raised his head. He looked scared. "Johnny'll kill me."

"You're going to prison." Reese let the words sink in. "What do you think will happen there?"

Fat T covered his face with one of his palms before lowering his hand and looking at Reese. "The man is bad news. He killed Hector and now he's come in and taken over Hector's territory. It's getting bigger all the time."

"That's nothing we don't already know," Reese said. "Tell me where he went."

Looking even more nervous, Fat T shook his big head. "He didn't say."

Reese clenched his jaw. "Tell me about the kids he's selling."

Fat T's jaw slackened. "I don't sell kids. Not me." He shook his head violently. "Never."

"You know that Johnny does." Reese narrowed his eyes. "And I'm getting damned tired of going in circles with you."

A deep inhale and then Fat T blew out his breath. "All I know is that he's getting a shipment together to send out next week."

"A shipment?" Reese wanted to lunge at the bastard and knock the information out of him. "You're talking about kids?"

Fat T licked his lips again. His voice was a croak. "He's been grabbing kids all over. Some in Flagstaff, some in Prescott Valley, most in Phoenix...but he even gets them off the Reservations."

The anger boiling inside Reese was threatening to erupt. He struggled to maintain his calm, not allowing Fat T to see exactly how the news was affecting him. He continued questioning Fat T, but didn't get much more out of him.

Ron Simpson provided even less information with regards to any elements of human trafficking, and refused to talk about the drug trafficking.

Frustration causing his whole body to ache, Reese strode out of the interrogation room that Simpson was being held in.

"Reese." John caught up with him. "The hard drive is being analyzed now and they've come up with some preliminary information."

They came to a stop, facing each other. "What've you got?" Reese asked.

John's expression was hard. "A couple of pictures of local missing women along with images of women being held captive. Also evidence of a website being pulled down. They're not finished."

"Sonofabitch." Reese blew out his breath, the heat of anger still boiling inside him. "We'll have to notify the FBI now that we know human trafficking is involved."

John gave a brief nod. "We sure will."

As Reese walked away from John, he rubbed his temples. He considered not telling Kelley what he'd learned, but she was his partner and he'd promised to tell her. He hadn't gathered enough information to pinpoint Johnny Rocha's or Taynor's locations so she wouldn't be running out the door the moment he told her.

Reese dragged his hand down his face then took his cell phone out of its holster and pressed the speed dial number for Kelley.

* * * * *

"You are too tense." Johan rested his hand on Kelley's good shoulder. "You need to relax."

"I can't." Kelley's mind had gone over and over what Reese had told her yesterday about the human trafficking and the drug bust, yet there were no concrete leads as to where Rocha and Taynor were.

Johan studied her. "Do you want to tell me?"

She met his gaze. She'd been coming regularly to physical therapy and she enjoyed talking with him. But this was something she didn't want to get into even if she had been able to talk about it.

"It's work related so I can't talk about it." She gave him a strained smile. "But thank you."

"I think you need a break." He tilted his head to the side as he looked her over. "Would you consider lunch at the Hummingbird? I get off work for lunch after your appointment."

Kelley nodded. "That sounds nice. I could use the distraction."

"Good." He started showing her another exercise. "A few more of these and then we can go."

When they finished, Kelley left to take her own SUV to the café where she would meet Johan. Her phone rang just as she reached the Explorer. She pulled it out of her pocket and checked the display to see that it was Reese. Heat traveled through her like it did every time she had any kind of contact with him these days.

She shook it off and answered the phone. "What's up, McBride?"

"Thought you might like to get out of the house for lunch," came his smooth, warm voice.

"I can't," she said. "I'm sorry."

"Don't be," he said. "I'll see you Sunday."

"Sunday?" Her brow wrinkled.

"Now who's forgetting our anniversary?" he said with amusement in his voice.

It had gone clean out of her mind. Still she said, "I was just testing you."

"Right." He gave a low laugh. "I'll pick you up at ten in the morning."

She opened the door to her SUV. "What are we doing?"

"I'm leaving it as a surprise." There was a note of mischief in his voice.

He'd never been playful with her in their roles as partners, and she found herself liking it. "How should I dress?"

"Jeans and a T-shirt," he said. "And hiking boots."

"Hmmm…" She thought about it as she climbed into her Explorer. "Are we going on a hike?"

"Not giving you any clues," he said. "Just be ready."

She felt like laughing for the first time in a while. "I'll be ready."

When she disconnected the call, she shoved the phone into her pocket and started the SUV.

It was only a five-minute drive from physical therapy to the Hummingbird. She parked in the back and walked around the corner to the front. While she waited for Johan, she went ahead and let the hostess seat her at a table on the patio. It was in the shade of the blue and white striped awning, the overhead misters cooling the air.

A few moments later, Johan arrived. She saw him walking up to the front entrance and she waved to him. He changed direction and came through the entrance into the wrought iron enclosure around the patio.

When he sat at the table, she smiled at him. For some reason she felt safe with him…like he wouldn't take advantage of their friendship and hit on her. She wasn't interested in any man. At least she was trying hard to convince herself of that fact.

Reese, her mind whispered to her and she had to shut the thought away.

Penny stopped by their table. She was the waitress who regularly worked the lunch crowd.

Kelley smiled. "Hi, Penny."

Penny set down a drink coaster for each of them. She smiled at Johan before saying to Kelley, "How're you doing, Detective?"

"Great." When it came to anyone outside of the police force, Kelley rarely gave indications that her day might be anything but good.

"Glad to hear that." Penny held her pen poised to write on an order pad. Kelley gave her drink order, as did Johan. "I'll be right back with your drinks."

When Penny left, Johan looked at Nectars, the bar next door to the Hummingbird. "The last time I was at Nectars, Stacy got jealous when someone hit on me." Johan shook his head and smiled. "It isn't easy being married to someone who's protective and has a jealous streak."

Kelley raised her brows. "I didn't realize you're married." She looked at his ring finger. "You're not wearing a ring."

"Stacy and I have been married for five years." Johan grinned. "I met him at the gym."

Kelley tried not to show her surprise that Johan was gay. No wonder she felt safe with him when it came to the opposite sex. "What does he do?" she asked.

Johan smiled. "He's an attorney at the law offices of Johnson and Hawk."

"Of course." She nodded. "Stacy Herrington. I didn't make the connection. He's been the defense attorney for a few trials I've been involved in." She gave Johan a little grin. "He's a nice guy for an attorney. Usually."

Johan grinned back. "True."

Penny arrived with their drinks. Kelley and Johan both knew what they wanted and Penny took their menus after she wrote down their sandwich orders.

"Have you been dizzy lately?" Johan asked after taking a drink of his iced tea.

"Better." Kelley shrugged. It was true…she hadn't had a spell all day today.

He nodded. "The doctor cleared you to drive?"

"Yes." She hadn't told the doctor about the occasional dizzy spell that she'd been having. "I can't wait 'til he clears me for work."

"Your strength is coming back, but I do not think it wise to go back to work just yet," he said.

She tried not to frown. "I hate sitting on the sidelines."

His expression turned serious. "Your body needs to heal."

With the same feeling of exasperation that she always felt when the subject was brought up, she pushed her fingers through her hair. "The case I should be working on…it's so important and could mean someone's life. I just can't sit and do nothing."

"Your partner, is he not qualified to handle this case?" Johan asked.

"Of course he is." She let out a sigh. "He's more than capable. But I should be there, too. With me on it, that gives us twice the manpower."

Penny returned with their sandwiches. "Here you go."

"That was fast," Kelley said, pleasantly surprised.

"Special for you, Detective, and your guest." Penny smiled. "Anything else for either of you?"

Both Johan and Kelley gave a shake of their heads. "No, but thank you, Penny," Kelley said.

As the waitress left, Kelley felt a prickling sensation crawl down her back, as if she was being watched.

She glanced across the street and saw Reese standing on the sidewalk next to his truck. He wore an unreadable expression. She'd raised her hand to wave when he turned and opened the door to the cab of his truck and climbed in. As far as she could tell, he didn't look in her direction as he drove away.

CHAPTER 10

A nervous twinge skipped through Kelley's abdomen as the doorbell rang. She brushed her palms over her jeans, tugged down her T-shirt, and touched her hand to her hair that was pulled back in a French braid. Her short lace-up leather hiking boots squeaked on the tile as she headed to the front door.

She put a smile on her face, took a deep breath, and opened the door. Reese stood on her doorstep, his hands shoved into the front pockets of his blue jeans. He wore a black T-shirt, a black ball cap with Arizona Diamondbacks emblazoned across it, and hiking boots similar to hers. No question about it, her partner was the most scrumptious man she knew—and she knew a lot of men.

His intense blue eyes met hers and a smile curved the corner of his mouth. "Ready, Petrova?"

She nodded. "Just a sec." She turned to the hall table and stuffed her wallet into the back pocket of her jeans and her phone in one of her front pockets then grabbed her keys. She shoved her holstered Glock into a hobo cross body purse, along with her belt. She made sure her hairbrush, lipstick, and a few other things were inside, then swung the purse over her shoulder. Reese waited for her on the porch as she locked the door with her keys then shoved them in her pocket.

They headed to his truck and he held the door open for her on the passenger side and she climbed in before he went to the driver's side and seated himself. He started the truck and it roared to life.

She tilted her head to the side. "So where are we going?"

"It's a surprise." He gave her a quick grin as he pulled away from the curb.

Even though he'd smiled, it seemed tense and she felt like something was off. "I saw you yesterday when I was having lunch with Johan. Why didn't you say 'hi'?"

Reese's expression tightened and he didn't look at her as he drove down the street. "Didn't want to disturb your lunch."

"You wouldn't have disturbed us." She studied him as he kept his eyes fixed on the street. "We were just talking." She continued to watch Reese as she said, "Johan is married to Stacy Herrington."

Reese glanced from the road to Kelley. "The attorney who works for Johnson and Hawk?"

She nodded. "That's the one."

He looked back at the road, his features lightening almost imperceptibly, as if her explanation somehow made him feel better. "How is PT going?"

Whether or not he wanted to admit it, Reese felt something for Kelley, like she did for him. She didn't know how much, but it was clear he'd been at least a little jealous until she'd told him Johan was married. The fact that Johan was gay probably made him less of a threat.

Less of a threat to what?

"Physical therapy is going well." She shifted in her seat as she answered his question. "My shoulder is getting better all the time. I hope the doctor will clear me to go back to work soon."

"No need to rush it," Reese said.

Kelley frowned. "Yes, there is a rush. We have to find Belle."

He met her gaze. "We will find her."

She glanced out the window to see they were headed out of town. "Are we going hiking?"

"Nope." He watched the road as he spoke. "I'll give you a hint. You're going to get dirty."

She tilted her head to the side. "Hmmm…I hope you're not planning on taking me to a mud bath."

His lips twitched but he shook his head. "Not even close."

She wracked her brain as they headed out onto Senator Highway and then she grinned. "The paintball arena."

"Very good, Detective." He returned her grin. "Thought you'd enjoy a little moving target practice."

"You know me well." She laughed. "I haven't been to the arena in ages."

Conversation was easy and natural with them as he drove, as if nothing between them had changed, as if the kiss had never happened. She decided not to ask about the case for now. She tensed at just the thought of it and today was about taking a break from life and enjoying themselves.

But Belle doesn't get to enjoy herself.

Kelley frowned at the thought. Guilt caused her gut to clench.

"What's wrong, Petrova?" Reese asked as he glanced at her. "I'd bet you're thinking about the case."

She sighed. "Like I said, you know me well."

He reached over the console and squeezed her hand. "You need a day to relax. You don't do that often enough."

She was going to argue with him that she'd done all the relaxing she wanted to do since she'd been on leave, but she decided she wouldn't argue and ruin the day. It was going to be hard enough to set aside thoughts of the case.

He let out his breath. "I'm just as guilty of not taking time off, but this is our two year anniversary as partners, and we're going to have a good time. Got it?"

She managed a smile. "Got it."

"Open the glove box." He nodded toward it.

She opened it and on top of the heap in the glove compartment sat a blue paper-wrapped package with a glittery blue bow. She glanced at him.

"Happy Anniversary." He gave a nod to the box. "Now open the package."

She picked up the box and put it into her lap as she looked at him. "You didn't have to get me anything."

"Just open it," he repeated.

Never one to be patient with unwrapping a package, she tore off the bow and ripped off the paper. "You're kidding," she said as she looked at a black plastic case. "You bought me a gun."

"You haven't even looked inside," he said with amusement.

She opened the case and her eyes widened. "A Glock."

He looked back at the road as he steered. "Latest model for women and I think the size and weight will work well for you."

"It's too much." She looked up from the case. "This cost a bundle."

"Nothing's too much for my favorite partner," he said.

She took the weapon out of the case and weighed it in her hand. "Feels nice. Different than my other Glock, but I like it."

He smiled. "Ammo is in the glove box."

She peered into the compartment and fished out the box of ammo then loaded the magazine before inserting it into the weapon. "It's great." She glanced at Reese. "Thank you."

"You're welcome." He pulled the truck off of the highway and onto the rough road that led to the arena.

As they arrived at the paintball arena, she tucked the weapon back in its case and into the glove box again. She dug into her purse and pulled out a package wrapped in gold paper with a gold bow.

After Reese parked, she handed him the gold package. He raised an eyebrow.

"Happy Anniversary," she said with a grin.

With a smile curving his lips, he tore open the package. It was a finely crafted pocketknife she'd picked up some time ago and had planned to give him for their anniversary since it had been coming up.

"This is great." He put his hand over hers and squeezed it. "Thank you."

She smiled and put her purse with her Glock into the center console where he left his own service weapon and the new pocketknife. He locked the glove compartment as well as the console and then they climbed out of the truck.

She had a feeling it was all he could do not to open up the truck door for her and help her out. He was giving her a different kind of respect as a cop because they were in public. He opened the back door to the cab on the driver's side and she joined him. He drew out two paintball guns, along with facemasks and paintballs. He also brought out two camouflage shirts with long sleeves, one small enough to fit her.

It was a beautiful day with a clear sky and a soft breeze. The air smelled sweet and clean.

When they were ready, Reese and Kelley headed up to the cabin where they checked in and were assigned to a team. Reese had made reservations earlier in the week.

"Oh, so not fair," came a female voice from behind them when they were putting on their red armbands to show they were on the red team.

Kelley and Reese turned to face Reese's cousin, Clint, who was with his new wife, Ella. It was Ella who'd spoken.

"Two detectives on the same team?" Ella shook her head. "Definitely not fair."

Reese grinned. "I seem to remember hearing you're a pretty damned good shot."

Ella shrugged and Clint put his arm around her shoulders. "She shoots almost as well as she sculpts."

"Then that's pretty damned good," Reese said as Ella gave him a hug.

"How are you two?" Kelley asked. "Enjoying wedded bliss?"

"We're doing great," Ella said with a stunning smile.

Reese nodded. "Ella made one hell of a beautiful bride."

Clint gave a proud smile. "She certainly did."

They chatted a little more as they stood in the dead zone. Their teams were called—Clint and Ella were on the blue team while Kelley and Reese were on the red team. Today's objective was to capture the flag at the center of a maze in the arena.

Adrenaline pumped through Kelley's body as she and Reese joined their team. It wasn't long before they were in the arena.

Kelley was determined to get the flag. She and Reese covered each other as they worked their way through the maze made up of bunkers and other structures. They picked off one opposing team member at a time. Kelley moved with smooth precision, her heart beating from the thrill of the hunt.

She had one near miss when a paintball splattered a foot from her arm. Her aim was true as she nailed her attacker in the chest.

As she rounded a structure, adrenaline kicked higher into gear. "There it is." She looked through her scope and saw a blue team member approaching the flag. She took aim and hit the player in the shoulder, above his heart.

When he turned his head, she saw that the player was Clint. He'd come close to taking the flag.

Reese and Kelley took out two more players who tried to capture the flag. When Kelley felt the coast was clear, she looked at Reese. "Cover me."

He gave a nod and she tore out into the open. She felt a paintball whiz by her ear but kept going. She heard a shout of "Damn," and thought that Reese must have nailed whoever had shot at her.

Another paintball hit the ground by Kelley's boot, splattering a little on the leather.

The flag was almost within her grasp. A blue team member charged out, trying to beat Kelley to the flag.

She was inches ahead, but she was shorter than her opponent. But she was also fast. She put on a burst of speed and dove for the flag.

With a triumphant shout, she clenched the yellow cloth in her hand as she surged to her feet and raised the flag.

The remaining red team members gave her high-fives and slaps on her back and she had to dodge a couple so that they didn't hit her shoulder.

Reese gave her a one-armed hug as they walked to the dead zone. "That's my girl."

She looked up at him and smiled. "Forget diamonds. This and the Glock are the best anniversary gifts a girl could get."

He laughed and released her. "Ready for another game?"

She gave an enthusiastic nod. "Absolutely."

They played two more games before quitting for the day. She and Reese hadn't captured the flag again, but they'd both made it through to the end of the games. Kelley's shoulder was sore, but she'd had more fun that she'd had in a long time.

"Thank you," she said as they walked back to the truck.

Reese stowed their gear. "I'm glad you enjoyed yourself."

"That I did." She stretched her arms over her head, easing out the kinks. "Best day ever."

He took the camouflage shirt from her after she stripped out of it. "Hungry?" he asked.

She held her hand to her belly. "Starving."

"I'll make dinner." He braced one hand on the truck. "My place isn't far from here."

"Okay." She nodded. After all this time being partners, she'd never been to his home. They'd worked together professionally and the only time they'd socialized had been when other officers were around, such as the Highlander, where a lot of firefighters and police officers preferred to hang out.

It was early evening when they pulled up to Reese's ranch home. A dog bounded away from the house and rushed up to the truck when Reese had parked. He'd already unlocked the center console and she took out her purse after he removed his own Glock. "We can leave your new Glock in the glove compartment. It's locked so it'll be safe," he said.

When Reese and Kelley were out of the truck, she slung on her cross body purse and he locked the truck.

He gave Ruff an affectionate pat. "Kelley, meet Ruff. Ruff, meet Kelley."

Ruff gave a doggy grin and bounced around as Reese introduced Kelley.

She held her hand out for Ruff to sniff and he pushed his nose beneath her palm so that she would pet him. "I see how you are," Kelley said to the dog whose one ear perked up while the other was flopped down. "You're a lover, aren't you?"

"He is," Reese said. "But he also makes a great watchdog as well as a good herder."

"What breed is he?" She looked at Ruff who had one green eye and one blue. "He looks like a mix breed."

"He's a mutt." Reese walked with Kelley to the front door of the house. "Best guess is he's got Australian Shepherd, Dalmatian, and probably Lab, too."

"He's a cutie, whatever he is," Kelley said.

"Don't let him fool you." Reese looked at the dog fondly even as he spoke. "He can be a big pain in the ass."

"Like some partners," she said with a grin.

Reese swatted her on the butt and she jumped and gave a little yelp of surprise. He winked and held the front door open for her.

Not sure what to make of her partner and his playfulness, she walked into the coolness of his home. She suddenly felt like she could use a good shower after their hours of play.

She looked around at the masculine décor and found that she liked what she saw. It had a comfortable lived-in feel to it. He told her she could leave her purse on the hall table. She set it down and then followed him into a kitchen with black appliances and dark green granite with black and gold flecks in it.

"You made dinner for me last time," she said. "Hardly seems fair if I don't do it this time." She hesitated, "Although that's only if you don't mind your food extra crispy or well-charred."

He grinned. "I've got it under control."

"I want to help." She leaned her hip against a counter as he opened the fridge. "What can I do?"

He rummaged around in the fridge and she watched as he pulled out a package of fresh salmon he'd obviously purchased from the grocery store, along with a lime and veggies.

Her stomach rumbled. "What are you making this time?"

"Grilled chili-lime salmon." He headed for a pair of arcadia doors off of the kitchen. "I'll fire up the grill."

She followed him and watched as he started a wood fire in an old-fashioned grill, including mesquite wood. Outside the weather was nice and she looked over his back yard. He had mostly desert landscaping with a few trees that towered above them, shading the porch and part of the backyard.

When they went back inside, Reese set to work. He looked so comfortable in the kitchen and she felt entirely inadequate as she offered to help again.

"I've got this." He nodded to the fridge. "Why don't you grab a couple bottles of beer?"

"That I can do." She opened the fridge and grabbed two bottles of Samuel Adams, then shut the door behind her with her hip.

He pointed her to the opener and she cracked open both bottles then handed one to him. "Happy Anniversary," he said and she repeated it as they clinked their bottles together. They both took a swallow.

Their eyes met and she thought for a moment that she wasn't going to be able to breathe. The way he was looking at her…

He turned back to preparing the salmon and she let her breath out in a rush. Having dinner with Reese in his home might not be such a great idea.

She took another drink of her beer. She wasn't driving so maybe she'd just get good and tipsy. Maybe then she'd be relaxed instead of worrying what tonight might bring.

What she wanted more than she was willing to admit.

She was grateful when she and Reese started into a conversation about the paintball games and the strategy they'd used or had seen used. Clint and Ella had come close to getting the flag once each, but they'd both been shot dead-on with paintballs.

When dinner was ready, she was on her second beer while Reese was still nursing his first. She felt a little reckless, wanting a closeness to him that only increased with every moment that passed. Dinner was wonderful but all she could think about was Reese and how much she wanted him. It was crazy and she knew better, but she couldn't help her wild thoughts.

After dinner, they cleaned the dishes and put everything away. Still feeling reckless, she opened up a third beer while he worked on his second. When they'd finished cleaning, she set her beer down on the counter and went to him.

His blue eyes looked dark and smoky, and she knew that he was feeling the same as she was. She took his beer from his hand and set it on the counter next to hers.

She reached up and wrapped her arms around his neck. His body felt warm and hard next to hers. He settled his hands at her waist, the heat of his touch traveling through her T-shirt. She smiled at him.

"Happy Anniversary," she said before rising up on her tiptoes and kissing him.

CHAPTER 11

Reese broke the kiss and Kelley found herself breathing hard as his gaze held hers. He cupped her face with one hand and brushed his thumb over her cheek. "You are something else, Kelley."

"What?" she asked, her voice low and breathy.

"You're so special to me." He lowered his head and their lips met again.

She could almost swear fireworks sparked behind her closed eyelids as he kissed her. It was a kiss like nothing she'd ever experienced before, a kiss she never wanted to end.

He scooped her into his arms, catching her off guard. She clung to his neck and he swept her out of the kitchen and down a hall, his stride long and deliberate. When he reached what she guessed was the master bedroom, he pushed the door open and set her on her feet on a hunter green rug next to a rustic four-poster bed. He swept aside the pillow from the top of the plaid comforter and pulled the comforter back with one hand.

Her insides tingled and then he was kissing her again while exploring her body with his fingertips. His touch was gentle when it came to her shoulder, but he pulled her tight up against him so that she felt the hard ridge of his erection against her belly.

He picked her up by her waist and set her on the edge of the mattress. She watched him, hunger growing within her as he knelt in front of her and tugged off one of her leather shoes and then the other. His gaze met hers as he peeled off each of her socks.

When her feet were bare, he caressed then before sliding his hands up her calves, over her jeans, on up to her thighs. The heat of his palms burned through the denim to her flesh. His hands continued on to the button of her jeans.

She couldn't take her eyes off him, her heart pounding faster with every movement he made. She braced her hands on the mattress and leaned back. Butterflies skittered through her belly as she raised her hips so that he could pull her jeans down.

Her breath caught in her throat as he removed her jeans, leaving her in her black panties. Still on his knees, he pressed his big body between her thighs, pushing them apart.

"Your skin is so soft." He skimmed his palms along her legs, causing goose bumps to rise up on her flesh. "I didn't know how much I wanted to touch you until this moment." His blue eyes held hers. "And now I don't think I can get enough."

She shivered as he said the words and he moved his hands over her hips, sliding over the silk of her panties to the hem of her white T-shirt.

"Is your shoulder going to be okay if we take this off?" he said as he paused.

She raised her arms. "My shoulder is fine now."

Still, he carefully eased the T-shirt over her head and arms. When the shirt was off, he set it aside, and he looked at her, taking in her black panties and matching satin and lace bra.

She bit her lower lip as he traced the line of her bra, skimming her breasts with his callused fingers. Her entire body grew sensitized, his every touch making her want him that much more.

He watched her as he cupped her breasts and ran his thumbs over her satin-covered nipples. They tightened and ached and she wanted nothing more than to feel the warmth of his mouth on them.

Unable to move her gaze from his, she arched her back, pressing her breasts against his palms. His eyes seemed to burn like blue flame as he reached behind her and unfastened her bra. He slid the straps down her arms and bared her breasts.

A low rumble rose up in his throat and he lowered his head and caught her nipple in his mouth. She gasped as he ran his tongue over the hardened nipple and then she sighed with pleasure. He slowly slid his lips from her nipple and down the mound to the valley between her breasts. He kissed the soft skin and moved his mouth up the other breast to the nipple and teased it with his tongue.

She slid her fingers into his light brown hair. The strands were silky to her touch and she gave a low moan as he teased one nipple with his fingers and another with his tongue. He raised his head, leaving her nipples damp and cool.

He studied her face then brought his mouth to hers, slowly kissing her as his fingers explored her body. She loved the way he kissed, the way their tongues met and he slid his into her mouth.

She brought her hands to his face and felt the day's stubble on his jaws beneath her palms. He kissed the corner of her mouth and kissed his way down her neck and to the hollow of her throat. He continued on, toward her injured shoulder.

He was far more gentle than she'd ever imagined he would be in his lovemaking. His touch was firing her up even more than she'd dreamed.

A feather-light touch of his lips skimmed the bullet wound and he kissed it softly. "I could have lost you." His voice sounded rough and he raised his head to meet her gaze. "I can't imagine life without you here."

Her throat constricted at his words. She tried to let them sink in but they seemed to skitter away as he reached for her panties. She braced her hands on the bed, raised her hips, and he slid them down to her feet.

Instead of tossing them aside, he brought them to his nose and inhaled. "You smell so good."

Wild sensations pinged through her body as he set her panties on the floor and pressed her thighs apart so that she was wide open and bared to him. He ran a finger over her shaved mound.

"I like this," he murmured as he touched the smooth skin. He continued on and skimmed her clit as he slid his finger down her wet folds.

Her eyes widened and her heart pounded harder against her ribcage as he stroked her slick flesh. Desire curled in her belly.

He got to his feet and she looked up at him, so tall as he towered over her. She swallowed as she watched him toe off his boots and then strip off his socks. He took his time, making her wait for him as he brought his hands to his belt and unfastened the buckle. She held her breath as he slid the leather from the belt loops.

The buckle thumped on the carpet when he dropped the belt. His top button was undone, but he didn't pull down his zipper.

He shrugged out of his overshirt and tossed it on top of the belt, leaving him in a T-shirt. He tugged the T-shirt over his head and her mouth watered at the sight of his muscles flexing as he stripped.

Now he was just in his Wrangler jeans. He watched her as he unzipped his jeans, revealing black boxer briefs. He pushed his jeans down and stepped out of them. His erection was huge behind the soft material of his boxer briefs. As he pushed them down, she couldn't take her eyes off of him.

The moment he released his cock and stripped out of his boxer briefs, she wanted to touch him, wanted to taste him. She slid off the bed and went to him. She wrapped her fingers around his cock and got down on her knees.

Reese hadn't expected Kelley to get down on her knees like this. He'd planned on giving pleasure to her, not taking for himself. But she had her fingers wrapped around his cock and she lowered her head.

She slid his cock into her mouth, bringing him deep to the back of her throat. He couldn't help but groan as she moved her wet mouth up and down his shaft. She swirled her tongue around the head of his cock before taking him deep again.

A throaty moan rose up in her as she bobbed her head up and down. He slid his fingers into her hair, stroking strands away from her face as she looked up at him. He could get lost in the depths of her blue eyes.

Her mouth was so warm on his cock. He couldn't remember ever feeling this way before. With Kelley it was so intense, so raw and filled with passion.

She made soft sounds of hunger and need as she sucked his cock. She moved her hands away from his erection, still bobbing her head. And then she was digging her nails into his ass.

The slight pain made the experience even more erotic and he groaned. That seemed to spur her on and she took him deeper yet.

He didn't think he could survive much more of the sweet torture she was inflicting on him. He pushed back the oncoming orgasm. He didn't want her to stop, but he wasn't going to be able to last much longer.

His gaze met hers again, and her eyes were dark with passion. An orgasm was rushing toward him and soon he would be powerless to stop it.

He leaned down and slid his fingers into her hair and he clenched the strands in his hands. "Stop." The word came out in a harsh tone. She let him slip his erection from her mouth and she gave him a smoky look filled with desire that he knew could lead into something fierce and primal if he let it go in that direction.

If it weren't for her shoulder, he would probably have acted like an animal, taking her too fast. "You make me crazy." His throat worked. "I want to take you hard and fast and out of control. But this is right…slow is the way you deserve to be taken."

She almost couldn't breathe as he bent and took her hands in his and helped her to her feet. When she was standing, she took his injured hand in hers and kissed the stubs where his fingers used to be. Her lips were soft against his skin.

When she raised her head again, he picked her up by her waist and laid her on the middle of the bed.

The tough, sometimes prickly female detective stared up at him and smiled, not looking so tough or prickly at all. She looked soft, warm, and inviting…and all his.

Kelley looked up at Reese in his masculine perfection. No, maybe not perfect in the Michelangelo's David sort of way, but perfect to her. The power of his presence, of his bearing. She'd known he was built well, but she'd never known just how well. His muscles were well defined but not too big…just right.

His cock, nestled in tight dark curls, was thick and long and she couldn't wait to feel him inside of her. He bent, picked up his jeans, and took his wallet out of his pocket. From his wallet he withdrew a foil packet, which he tossed on the bed before dropping his wallet on top of his jeans.

She held out her arms to him and he moved toward her. He eased onto the bed and knelt between her legs before pushing her thighs wide apart with his hands. While he watched her face, he slid two fingers into her moist core. Her eyes widened as he thrust his fingers in deep, down to his knuckles. He placed one hand on her knee as he moved his fingers out, ran them along the length of her folds and then slipped them inside her core again.

"Please." The word came out with a hoarse edge to it. "I want you inside me."

His smile was so carnal, so filled with passion, that she caught her breath. "Not yet."

He lowered himself so that his shoulders were between her thighs, his face close to her sex. He blew lightly on her clit and she nearly came up off the bed.

Before she had a chance to recover from the zing that had shot straight through to her belly, he shifted so that his face was close to her folds. He slid his fingers inside her at the same time he licked her clit.

A cry caught in her throat and she gripped the sheet in her fists as if that might hold her to the bed. She felt like she could go flying at any moment and he had barely started.

Her body felt like it was on fire, her legs trembling with the need to climax. He slowly licked and sucked her while slowly moving his fingers in and out.

An orgasm built and built within her. Perspiration broke out on her body and she was fighting to remain grounded, like she might fly into pieces that could never be put back together again.

He made a low rumbling sound against her folds and she lost it. She cried out loud and long. It was like a bubble burst around her and she was set free, floating up into the night sky. He continued licking her, as she floated but then her body tensed and from out of nowhere another orgasm slammed into her. She twisted in his grasp, no longer able to take any more of his tongue on her clit.

As she came back down to earth, she felt the heat of him against her as he eased up on top. She loved the feel of his hard body as he pressed it to hers. He braced his hands to either side of her shoulders, holding most of his weight off of her.

He lowered his head and brought his mouth to hers. She wrapped her arms around his neck as he kissed her, a hard, intense kiss that made her heart skip a beat. He rose up and braced himself with one hand while grasping his cock in his other and pressing it against her core. She looked to see that he'd put on a condom, likely when she was in the middle of her massive orgasm.

She gasped as he pushed his way inside her. He moved slowly but he was so big and she was so petite that it almost hurt as he stretched and filled her. But at the same time it felt so incredible that what little pain she'd felt vanished.

He began moving in and out of her and she rose up to meet his every thrust. She'd never felt anything like having him inside her, his body pressed to hers. His skin was hot and she felt their perspiration mingling as he took her.

His thrusts grew harder and faster and it felt as if he was going deeper with each movement. She watched the intensity in his fierce expression, the set of his jaw and the wildness in his blue eyes. She had no doubt that he was close to coming.

Her own orgasm came closer and closer. She felt fire burning through her body again and knew it wouldn't be much longer…

"Come for me, honey." He said the words in a growl.

She completely lost it. She cried out again as her mind seemed to spiral and her body vibrated. Her core spasmed around his cock and a beat later he gave a loud shout. She watched him as he came, loving how he looked as he lost control.

He thrust in and out several more times and then he rested his big frame against her. She loved the feel of his body and didn't want him to move, but then he was rolling onto his side, taking her with him. He tucked her head in the crook of his arm and held her close.

She sighed, pleasure filling her from head to toe. A smile touched her lips and she wanted to tell him how good he'd just made her feel.

And how much he meant to her. But she wasn't ready for that. She wasn't even ready to admit to herself how she cared about him in ways she had never cared for anyone before him.

She snuggled closer. For now she wanted to feel happy, secured, and cared for. They both let the moment fill them as if neither one of them wanted to disturb the beauty that had just happened between them.

CHAPTER 12

Kelley felt like she was floating in a soft cocoon. She breathed deeply, filling her lungs, smelling clean sheets and a warm masculine scent. She felt heat, like she was lying in a pool of sunshine.

She opened her eyes to see Reese on his side, his elbow on the bed and his head propped on his hand. The sheet draped his hips, showing tantalizing muscles and his athletic form. His brown hair was tousled but he looked wide-awake as he watched her.

She smiled. "Good morning." A hint of sleepiness was still in her voice.

"You look beautiful when you sleep." He brushed his fingers from her shoulder to her elbow and back. "You're always beautiful."

Warmth traveled through her. "Any regrets?" she asked.

"None." He leaned closer and kissed her forehead then drew back. "You?"

She reached up and stroked his stubble with her fingertips. "Not one."

"Good." He moved his hand to her hair, tucking strands of it behind her ear. "Hungry?"

"Famished." She moved her hand from his jaw to her belly. "I wouldn't mind a nice big breakfast."

"A girl after my own heart." He kissed her forehead again before scooting up and sliding out of bed. She watched him, the sheet falling from his body and revealing every glorious inch of his large frame. She wouldn't mind having more of that right now.

He looked amused. "If you're not careful and keep looking at me like that, we'll never get to breakfast."

She grinned. "Is that such a bad thing?"

He gave her a quick grin. "Better watch yourself, Detective Petrova."

She gave him a sultry look. "What if I don't want to watch myself?"

His features turned hungry, his eyes filled with desire. He went to her, pulled the covers away, and slid back into bed.

After another round of satisfying lovemaking, Reese slid out of bed. "I'm going to take a shower."

"I'll be right there." She sighed, looking entirely content lying in his bed, her breasts and torso bared to her waist.

She wandered into the bathroom as he was pulling on boxers and Wrangler jeans. He kissed her and headed out of the bedroom. When he reached the kitchen, he started a pot of coffee first off. Then he grabbed ingredients for homemade biscuits from the pantry as well as raided the fridge for hamburger to make hamburger gravy, and then took out a carton of eggs. He started browning the hamburger then mixing the ingredients for biscuits.

It wasn't long 'til Kelley made it to the kitchen. She wore one of his button-up shirts. She was so petite that the shirt was almost to her knees. Her phone was in the breast pocket and her legs were bare as she padded across the floor.

"Mmmm…smells wonderful," she said. "Especially the coffee." Her blonde hair was damp from the shower and she had a rosy glow about her. "What can I do to help?"

"You can stand there looking beautiful," he said with a smile.

She went to him and reached up and kissed his cheek. "What's for breakfast?"

"Entirely unhealthy grub." He gestured to the pan of gravy he was making. "Biscuits, hamburger gravy, and fried eggs."

"Yum." She moved back and leaned against the counter. "I'd offer to crack the eggs, but we'd be having broken yolks mixed with the egg whites and shells."

He gave a low chuckle. "I'll handle it."

She eased herself up so that she was sitting on the counter, her legs dangling and the shirt hiked up to her upper thighs. Damn, she looked good.

Her forehead wrinkled. "How and when are we going to tell our superiors that we're in a relationship?" She hesitated. "Or maybe I'm assuming too much since we've only been together for one night?"

He set down the spoon that he'd been using to stir the gravy and went to her. He braced his hands to ether side of her hips on the countertop. "You're damned straight we're in a relationship." He moved in closer and brushed his lips over hers. "You belong to me now."

She swatted his shoulder. "You know better than to play He-man with me."

He grinned. "You're so damned cute when you're riled."

With a sniff she said, "You haven't seen riled yet."

His grin broadened. "I'll be sure and be on my best behavior."

She gave him a teasing look. "That's no fun."

He kissed her hard before moving back to the stove. "The gravy is going to burn."

"Can't have that." She jumped down from the countertop. "I'll set the table."

While he stirred the gravy, with his free hand he gestured to a cabinet. "Plates there." He pointed to a drawer. "Silverware in that drawer." He nodded to a napkin holder. "And napkins."

While he made breakfast, he glanced at her as she got everything out and set the table. She then grabbed the Red Devil hot sauce out of the fridge along with butter and honey if they wanted a biscuit without the gravy on it. She put shakers of salt and pepper on the table, too.

While he made breakfast they talked about his family and coworkers, and somehow managed to stay off the topic of the Taynor case. Talking about the case they were working on was inevitable, but for now they seemed to be in agreement that they weren't going to get into it, at least not until after they ate.

Breakfast went smoothly, but afterward as they started putting everything away and cleaning up, Kelley brought up the case.

"I'm feeling better." Kelley dried a washed plate as he cleaned the silverware. "I'm sure the doctor will clear me soon, so it won't hurt for me to work on the case."

"Don't push yourself, honey." He glanced at her and her eyes widened a little, as if he'd surprised her by calling her honey. "You need to get back to full speed."

She put the dry plate into the cabinet and frowned. "How many times am I going to have to tell you I'm fine?"

"At least a hundred until the doctor says you're ready for duty." He set the clean silverware down to be dried.

"You didn't answer the question I asked you in regards to telling our superiors about our relationship." She looked a little more serious and a little sad. "They won't allow us to be partners any longer."

He gave a slow nod. "We'll need to do it before you go back to work."

"Which will be soon," she said.

He remained quiet. No way was he going to come out on top of this argument with Kelley. She was too fierce, independent, and stubborn as hell. They were qualities he admired in her—they made her one hell of a detective. But they also led to frustration when it came to getting her to slow down or stay put when she needed to. Like now.

"Something's got to break." She dried the silverware and tucked them into the drawer. Her brows narrowed. "We have to find them before they manage to get out of Prescott." She looked at Reese. "No way is Taynor going to hang around town with every law enforcement officer in the state looking for him." She frowned. "Unless he's waiting for something to go down…"

Reese nodded. She had good instincts and he happened to agree with her in this instance.

Just as Kelley dried her hands off with a towel, her phone rang in the breast pocket of the shirt. She pulled it out and looked at the caller ID. "It's Zip."

Reese couldn't help a frown. If she got another lead on Taynor or Rocha, she'd be tearing after them before he could say "whoa."

She answered with, "Detective Petrova." For a moment she listened, her features grim. "I'll meet you there in fifteen. Detective McBride will be with me." She disconnected the call.

Reese dried his own hands. "What's up?"

She looked grim. "Zip sounded almost scared. He wants to meet at our usual place." She turned and headed out the kitchen toward Reese's bedroom and he followed.

When he reached his room, Kelley was shoving her legs into her jeans. "Ugh. After playing outside all day yesterday, I need clean clothes. These have paint splatters from near misses." She turned to face him as she grabbed her T-shirt and pulled it over her head. "After we see Zip we can go to my place."

Reese nodded as he tugged on a T-shirt and then an overshirt before strapping on his belt and holstering his Glock and phone.

After she'd put on her hiking boots and he'd stuffed his feet into his western boots, they headed out of the room. Kelley grabbed her purse. "Looking forward to using the new Glock," she said as she glanced at him. "That is a hell of a firearm."

He smiled and rested his hand on her shoulder as they walked out the door of his bedroom. "I'm glad you like it."

"How could I not?" She grinned up at him as they reached the hall table where she'd left her purse. She pulled out her weapons belt and her new sheathed Glock that she'd taken out of the glove compartment earlier.

When she was finished, they headed out the front door. "Thank you for not getting one in pink."

He locked the door behind them. "I know better. No pink or paisley for you."

She shook her head and grinned. "Nope."

Kelley waited as Reese hit the remote for his truck locks and she let him open the passenger door for her. Her thoughts filled with meeting Zip, she climbed into the cab and Reese shut the door behind her.

It wasn't long before they were headed off to the abandoned ranch to meet with her informant. The drive was short and when they arrived, Zip was already there, leaning against his blue Camaro, smoking a cigarette. As Kelley climbed out of the truck, he pushed away from the car, tossed his cigarette down and ground it into the dirt with his shoe.

Kelley walked the distance between the truck and Zip. "What do you have to tell me?" she asked.

Zip shoved his hands in his front pockets, darting a nervous glance at Reese before looking at Kelley again. "Johnny Rocket has a shipment ready to send down to Mexico."

Kelley frowned as thoughts raced through her mind. "Why would he be shipping drugs to Mexico?"

"Not drugs." Zip shook his head. "Women. Girls. He's selling them into slavery and they're being sent to South America. Apparently he has wealthy clients who like blonde hair and blue eyes. *Gringas.* Johnny's been kidnapping them from all over Northern Arizona and he trades them for cocaine."

Kelley tried not to reveal her shock in her expression. "Where is his 'shipment' of women and girls?"

Zip pushed his fingers through his hair looking distracted, his body seeming to vibrate as if he was high on crack. It was hard to tell if it was fear or if it was drugs that made him act this way.

"If he finds out I tipped you off, he's going to kill me." Zip's hands shook as he took a lighter and another cigarette out of his pocket.

"I can get you protection, Zip," Kelley said.

He shook his head. "I'd rather take my chances."

She flexed her fingers, her whole body wired for action. "Where are they?"

Zip lit the cigarette, took a hit on it, and blew out the smoke. She thought she was going to lose it as she waited for him, her patience riding on a thin line.

He lowered the cigarette. "In the back of a semi. It's ready to leave soon."

"He has the girls in the back of a semi?" Kelley's mind spun. "In this heat?"

"Where?" Reese's voice jarred Kelley as he repeated her question. She was so wrapped up in Zip's revelation that for a moment she'd forgotten Reese was there.

Zip answered, giving them an address that wasn't too far from the warehouse that had been blown up not that long ago, the one that had taken Reese's two fingers and had given her the concussion.

"If this pays off, I'll give you your usual fee," she said as she and Reese hurried back to the truck.

"Double it," Zip called after her.

She didn't answer. Instead, she climbed into the truck as Reese called for backup.

CHAPTER 13

Sirens wailing and lights flashing, Reese and Kelley tore through Prescott in his truck. She clenched and unclenched her hands, praying that Zip had given her the right information and that they'd get there before Rocha's shipment of women and girls left town.

Shipment. A part of her couldn't believe that this was going on in their town. It seemed almost inconceivable. Bad things went on everywhere, but slavery was something that just didn't happen in this area.

Hadn't happened, she corrected herself. With this news, everything had changed.

That bastard, Johnny Rocha, had brought bad things to Prescott. Seriously bad things, worse than what they'd been facing before.

Reese cut the sirens when they closed in on the location Zip had given them. They pulled onto the street, not too far from where a semi truck was parked in front of an old condemned building.

The ground around the building was barren with sporadic patches of weeds and yellowed grass.

He parked his truck and climbed out at the same time Kelley did. From behind the front seat, he brought out a bulletproof vest and his raid jacket with POLICE across the back. He was all business now. Gone was the friend and lover, something she appreciated even if she didn't appreciate his over-concern.

"I don't have a vest small enough to fit you." He frowned. "You need to stay with the truck."

She clenched her jaw, giving him a stubborn look. "I'm in on this, Reese. It's my informant, my tip."

"Damn it." He looked away as two police cruisers came down the street. When he returned his gaze to her, he said, "Wear my jacket."

She would have laughed if the situation weren't so dire. She shook her head. "It'll go down to my knees."

Police cruisers arrived from both sides of the street, blocking incoming and outgoing traffic. Officers also went around the back so that both entrances to the building were covered.

Just as the team started to approach the semi and the building, the big rig roared to life. A man appeared in the driver's seat, as if he'd been lying down and was now straightening behind the wheel. Kelley saw his arm move and heard gears grinding.

Officers in front of the truck positioned themselves so that their vehicles shielded them. Their guns were trained on the driver.

"The girls could be in the back of that truck." Kelley narrowed her gaze as she looked at the vehicle then glanced at Reese. "If we're going to take him out, we've got to do it now, before that truck starts moving."

Reese gave a nod. He spoke into his radio and divided his team into three. One team to penetrate from the back of the building, one team to enter through the front entrance, and a team for the truck.

On Reese's signal, the teams went into action. Shouts of "Police!" rang through the air along with gunfire the moment the two teams entered the house.

Reese and Kelley were with the team that was prepared to take the truck. Reese had his weapon ready. Like Reese, Kelley had her gun trained on the truck driver. The man's window was open, so Kelley knew he had to hear every word they said.

"Step out now with your hands up," Reese shouted as he eased closer to the driver's side door. "We *will* shoot."

The truck motor roared. Kelley saw the fierceness in the driver's eyes and in his expression.

"He's not going to surrender," Kelley said.

Reese gave a nod to one of the snipers. "Take him out."

The truck vibrated as if the driver was shifting into gear.

A crack from a rifle. A hole appeared in the driver's forehead and his eyes went blank. He slumped over the wheel.

The rig started to roll.

Reese bolted the few feet to the truck. He jumped onto the running board and wrenched open the door of the cab.

The truck crept slowly forward as he hung on with the three fingers of his left hand and grabbed the dead man by his collar with his opposite hand. He pulled the man's body out of the cab and it tumbled to the ground.

Kelley's heart beat faster as the semi slowly picked up speed, heading toward the line of vehicles in front of it.

Reese swung inside the cab. He wrangled for control of the truck as it got closer and closer to the police cruisers. Officers jumped clear as the huge semi plowed into the vehicles.

Metal crunched. Glass shattered. Brakes screeched.

And then moments later, the truck came to a shuddering stop. Reese killed the engine and the rumble died away.

Even though she'd been concentrating on the semi, she'd also been aware of what was apparently going on in the building. Whoever had been inside had put up a fight, but now the teams that had taken the building were marching cuffed men outside.

Reese and Kelley both ran to the back of the semi trailer. A large padlock was on the back, locking the doors tightly. Reese called out for bolt cutters.

Kelley's heartbeat was erratic as she waited to see what was in the back of that trailer. Would Belle be there? What about the women Zip had claimed were in the back of a semi? Was this the right one?

In moments, an officer had returned with bolt cutters. John came up beside Reese and Kelley as they waited for the lock to be cut. The lock dropped to the ground and both Reese and John climbed up and opened the trailer's doors.

Kelley's breath stuck in her throat as she saw eight women and girls bound and gagged. They looked terrified, as if suffering from heat exhaustion, and faint with hunger, even as they blinked away the sudden brightness from outside.

"We're the police." Reese walked into the trailer. "You're all safe now."

Looks of relief crossed some faces, disbelief on others. Tears rolled down many of the women's and girls' cheeks.

Kelley climbed inside. The hot interior reeked with smells of sweat and unwashed bodies. She recognized several from pictures that had been circulated of each missing woman or girl from missing persons cases. How long had some of them been gone from their families?

While she walked through the back, stepping over many of the occupants, all appearing to be blonde and blue-eyed, Kelley made reassuring comments as she went. With single-minded determinedness, she searched for Belle.

"I can't find her." Kelley fought to keep her voice calm. "I can't find Belle."

"I don't see her, either," Reese said as he knelt and began freeing the occupants by cutting their bonds and then removing their gags.

Louder sobs and whimpers could be heard now that gags were being removed. Officers helped women out of the back of the trailer. Grateful words were being said by many of the women while others looked too shell-shocked to speak.

Sirens approached, no doubt ambulances. Some of these women could be transported in available vehicles to the hospital, but others needed immediate care.

Kelley still kept her eyes open in case Belle was here, but her heart sank even further when she didn't see the girl anywhere.

"Petrova." John's voice had Kelley turning to face the truck's opening. "You need to see this."

Kelley finished freeing a girl then helped her to the back of the truck. When they reached it, Kelley handed off the girl to a paramedic.

"What do you have?" Kelley asked John.

John inclined his head to where Reese was now standing and holding a blood-splattered document. Kelley felt a renewed pounding in her chest.

"What is it?" Kelley asked as she reached him.

He raised his head. "John took this off the dead driver. It's a bill of sale to someone named Ortega." He handed the papers to Kelley, his features hard. "These women were being sold like cattle."

Her stomach churned and bile rose in her throat. "We've got to get to Johnny Rocha." The paper wrinkled in her hand as she clenched it. "I'll kill him myself."

"If I don't get to him first," Reese said in a growl.

Chapter 14

Sometime later, after things had been sorted out and the women and girls whisked to the hospital, Reese took Kelley to her home. Unbelievably, it was only two in the afternoon. It was hard to believe that only that morning she'd awakened in Reese's bed and had enjoyed breakfast with him before Zip called. Everything from that point had tumbled from one thing to another.

She was so wound up that when she looked at Reese, she felt a need so great for him that she could barely keep from touching him. She clenched and unclenched her fists. God, she had to have him.

When they reached her home and Reese parked, Kelley looked at him. "You are coming inside," she stated.

He looked at her, his eyes darkening with arousal. She hurried out of the truck and he walked with her to the front door. She fished her keys out of her purse and unlocked the door.

When they were inside and had closed the door behind them, he grabbed her by the waist and she gasped as he slammed her up against the wall. His mouth came down hard on hers and she groaned as he kissed her with savage need.

She let her purse drop to the floor with a loud thump. He drew away long enough to pull her T-shirt over her head, taking care not to hurt her shoulder, but stripping her bare all the same. He dropped the shirt and unfastened her bra before tossing it aside.

With a growl of need, he lowered his head and sucked her nipples. She moaned, wanting to climb him, wanted him inside her.

She pushed his overshirt off and he let it fall to the floor, then he helped her tug his T-shirt over his head. And then they were bare chest to bare chest as they kissed with frantic abandon.

"Where's your room?" he asked in a husky voice. He'd been to her home before, but never to her bedroom.

"I don't want to wait." She had a hard time getting the words out, she was so anxious to be with him. "I want you now."

Her words seemed to incite him even more. He swung her around and set her on the sofa before going down on a knee and removing her boots and socks. He brought her to her feet again and shoved her jeans down to her feet and she stepped out of them.

He moved her up against the wall again as he paused long enough to fish a foil packet out of his wallet and then tossed the wallet aside. He unbuckled his belt and unzipped his jeans before pushing his jeans and boxers down and freeing his erection. He tore open the packet and quickly sheathed his cock.

With a groan, he lifted her up by her ass and she wrapped her legs around his hips, feeling his erection against her. He positioned himself at the entrance to her core and slammed his cock inside of her.

She nearly screamed at the suddenness and pleasure of his entry. He took her mouth again as he fucked her hard and fast. She hung on for dear life. The wall was hard against her back, his kiss fierce. She matched him with her own hungry kiss.

An orgasm rushed forward, and her head seemed to spin. He pulled away and he watched her as she came. Sparks exploded in her mind as her orgasm slammed into her. She screamed.

He took her harder and harder yet, his expression primal as she climaxed again. Her core pulsed around his cock and then he was shouting his release. She felt the throb of his cock inside her as he moved in and out a few more times.

A groan rumbled out of him as he sagged against her, pinning her to the wall. Both of them were breathing hard, perspiration coating their skin. He kissed her again before raising his head.

He took only long enough to pull his jeans up to his hips, and then with his eyes fixed on hers, he took her down to the rug and brought her into his arms. She sighed and rested her head against his chest. His embrace felt secure and she melted more fully against him. He smelled of sun-warmed flesh and his bare chest was hard against her cheek.

For a moment she wondered why she didn't mind showing any kind of weakness in front of him now. Their relationship had changed irrevocably and with it, so had her need to hide anything from Reese.

When she tilted her head back to look into his eyes, he was studying her. He lowered his mouth and kissed her long, sweet and slow.

He drew away, breaking the kiss, and brushed hair from her eyes with his fingers. "I don't know how long I can be your partner without worrying about you."

She frowned. "We've been partners for a long time. You know I can take care of myself."

He gave a gentle smile. "Yes, you can. I've never doubted that."

She moved her hands to his chest. She liked the feel of his bare skin against her palms and how his body heat radiated through her. "Then what's the problem?"

"I—" he started say but his cell phone rang and he paused.

"Go ahead." She let her hands slide away from his chest. "Take the call."

He sat up and unholstered his cell phone. "Detective McBride," he answered. As he listened to the caller, his expression darkened. "I'll be right there."

"What happened?" she asked as he holstered his phone.

"Your informant, Zip." Reese looked grim. "He's been found. Dead."

CHAPTER 15

"Zip has been murdered?" A cold chill washed over Kelley's skin. "Where?"

"In his apartment." Reese pushed his fingers through his hair. "Neighbors heard shots and called the police. When they arrived they found his body."

"I'm going to the scene." She scrambled to her feet. "I just need to get on some clean clothes."

Reese looked like he was going to say something, but thankfully he didn't.

She hurried to her room and changed into clean panties, bra, jeans, and T-shirt. At least she'd showered that morning. Having met with Zip and then immediately investigating his lead, she hadn't had a chance to go home and get into clean clothes until now.

When she returned to the living room, she scooped up her cross body purse from where she'd dropped it on the floor. Reese reached for the doorknob, opened the door, and held it so that she could walk through. She locked the door behind him as he stepped out of the way.

As she shoved her keys into her purse, she hurried down the steps to his truck to keep up with his long strides. Within moments they were in the vehicle and driving to the part of town where Zip lived.

She felt jittery, as if she'd had a dozen cups of coffee. Had someone found out that Zip had given her the lead to the women and girls? Or had he been murdered for some other reason? Damn, she should have made him accept the protection.

When they arrived, squad cars were parked in front of the apartments, the vehicle's red and blue emergency lights flashing. The area was cordoned off with yellow tape.

Kelley and Reese climbed out of his truck and met up with John.

John glanced toward the first floor apartment door where law enforcement personnel were going in and out. He looked at Kelley and Reese. "No sign of forced entry or struggle. The victim may have known his assailant, but so far we haven't been able to determine if that was the case."

Kelley nodded. "Anything else?"

"It wasn't clean," John said. "He was shot in the gut and he bled out."

Kelley felt a moment's pity. Zip hadn't been an upstanding citizen, but he hadn't deserved to die like that.

"Any witnesses?" Reese asked John.

John gestured to a woman speaking with a uniformed officer. "She heard shots then looked out her window in time to see a vehicle fleeing the scene. It was an older rusty pickup truck, but that's all she could tell us. Using her description, we've got an APB out on the vehicle. No one seems to have seen anyone coming out of the victim's apartment."

"You're sure the victim is Zip?" Kelley asked.

John gave a single nod. "Yeah, it's him."

"Thanks, John." She turned to Reese. "Let's check it out."

They entered the apartment that was being looked over from top to bottom. Zip's body was face down, but his head was turned to the side so that Kelley could see his bloodless face. There was a path of blood behind him, as if he'd dragged himself this far, and a pool of blood beside him.

She shook her head and cut her gaze to Reese. "Do you think he was killed for tipping us off about the shipment of women and girls?"

"Could be." Reese took a pair of disposable gloves out of his pocket and Kelley dug a set out of her purse.

Reese and Kelley worked their way through the apartment. He picked up a cell phone near the location where Zip's body lay. Reese scrolled through recently called numbers.

"Here's your number." He paused then scrolled to the next one. "Look at the date and time stamp. Someone called him around the same time we found the victims."

"Look." She knelt. A corner of a piece of paper, wet with blood, was sticking out from beneath Zip's body. "Help me move him so that I can get the paper out."

Carefully, Reese raised the body. Zip's hand that had been pinned beneath his body was clenching a pen. Kelley pulled the paper out that was half covered with blood and bloody fingerprints.

There was writing that was legible on a portion of the paper that wasn't coated in red.

"He had enough in him to write his killer's name and give us a message." Kelley raised the bloody paper in her glove-covered hand as she read the shaky writing aloud.

> *Rocket shot me*
> *Hurt Petrova*
> *Girl to border soon*
> *Brown car*
> *Douglas*

The last word was barely legible, the handwriting trailing off so that the tail of the S went halfway down the page, into the blood.

"Johnny Rocha's taking Belle to Douglas and plans to cross the border with her." Kelley looked at Reese.

With a frown, Reese stood and called to John. Kelley got to her feet, too, fury welling up inside her.

John reached them and Reese gestured to the paper. "Contact all law enforcement agencies between here and Douglas. We've got to get this guy before he crosses the line with the girl." Reese glanced back at the paper. "Be on the lookout for a brown car."

John nodded. "I'll take care of it," he said before he turned and headed away from them. He raised his radio and spoke into it as he walked.

"We've got to go after him." Kelley narrowed her eyes at the paper again.

"Rocha plans to hurt you." Reese's jaw tightened. "We've got to get you someplace safe."

"How's he going to do that?" She shook her head. "He's on the run."

"He must have something planned." Reese gave her a hard look. "We can't take chances."

"You're not taking me out of action." Kelley bristled, her entire body going tense. "Either I head south with you, or I go alone."

Reese said nothing as they walked out the door of the apartment and into the sunny afternoon. "My truck needs fuel," he said after they were in the vehicle and he started it.

Kelley pushed her hair out of her face in frustration. "We've got to hurry."

Still frowning, he drove to the closest gas station. As Reese fueled the tank, Kelley slipped on her cross body purse, then went inside the convenience store and used the restroom. When she walked out of the restroom, Reese was inside, paying the cashier for four large bottles of water and several packages of snacks.

"For the road." He took the bags off the counter. "We missed lunch."

She nodded. With all that had happened, she'd forgotten about food.

They hurried out to the truck and in moments were headed out of town. The first light they came to changed red and Reese applied the brakes.

The truck didn't slow down. Reese pumped the brake pedal. "I've lost the brakes."

Kelley's heart pounded as they hurtled toward the intersection. He tried setting the emergency brake but the truck kept moving.

"Hang on," he said through gritted teeth.

Kelley braced herself as they barreled into the intersection at full speed just as a semi drove in front of them.

With horror she prepared herself for impact.

Reese's truck slammed into the semi. Metal crunched, glass shattered, Kelley screamed.

The semi jackknifed. Reese's truck whipped around and then rolled. Everything spun as the truck flipped over and over.

It came to a halt then rocked before it stopped. The whole world seemed to have collapsed.

Disoriented, Kelley realized she was hanging upside down, held in her seat by her seatbelt. She put her hand to her forehead and felt slick blood flowing from a laceration on her temple.

Smells of burning rubber and gasoline were strong and she heard the slow plink of something dripping. Fuel? Tires screeched close by and she heard voices.

She tried to focus as she turned her head to look at Reese who was hanging upside down, motionless. The steering wheel had been crammed up tight to him. Blood coated the side of his face.

"Reese!" She felt like her head was spinning as she fumbled for her seat belt. She had to get to him. When she found the release she pressed the button and then fell hard from the seat to the shattered window. Her head struck metal and glass and her body cried out in pain.

For a moment she could only lie there, trying to stop the dizziness. Before she could reach for Reese, she heard the sound of metal against metal. Someone tried to wrench the passenger door open but it wouldn't budge. She looked at the shattered window. A face came into view.

Taynor.

Kelley reached for her gun but it wasn't in its holster. In the next moment, Taynor grabbed her feet and jerked her out through the window.

Glass cut into her body but she barely felt it as she fought to get away from Belle's murdering kidnapper. Woozy and weak, she tried kicking, but he had a tight grip on her ankles. She grabbed at the seatbelt in an effort to hang on to something, but Taynor jerked hard and dragged her completely out of the truck.

A car was parked beside the truck, the back door open. Taynor threw Kelley onto the floorboard and she hit her head on the opposite side of the car. Her head spun and once again she felt disoriented and unable to form coherent words. She shifted, trying to sit, but ended up curling her body so that she lay on one side of the hump on the floorboard.

She was vaguely aware of Taynor sliding into the backseat and slamming the door shut. She tried to move but he had rope and tied her wrists and then ankles together before she could think to struggle. He leaned over her, a satisfied look on his features, and she saw that he was holding her Glock. He stuffed the weapon in the back of his jeans then put a handkerchief in her mouth and tied the ends behind her head.

Tires screeched and the car fishtailed as it left the intersection and took off. She fought to focus as she blinked and looked up.

Taynor stared down at her, a leer on his twisted features. "You're going to pay, bitch. You're the one who convinced Laura to leave me, and you're the one who found the shipment."

Kelley's head throbbed as she narrowed her gaze at him, unable to speak with the gag in her mouth.

"But now I'll get even with you." His smile made her skin crawl. "It was Johnny's idea to put a tracker on that asshole detective's truck. It was my idea to disable the brakes when we followed the truck and you stopped to gas it up and went into the convenience store. Being a mechanic comes in handy." His gaze traveled from her face and rested on her breasts. He met her gaze again. "It was Johnny's idea to sell you to a buyer in South America. It won't make up for the shipment you cost us, but you'll bring top dollar."

Her skin went cold. They intended to sell her?

Over my dead body.

She couldn't see anything they passed from her awkward position on the floorboard, but a good fifteen minutes had passed before she felt the vibration and heard the thrumming when the car rattled over a cattle guard. The road became bumpy, jarring her and causing pain to clench her body as they were clearly driving down a dirt road. The smell of dust came in through the open window. They had to be somewhere in the country.

As her captors drove her, she thought of Reese. He'd been so still and all that blood… Was he alive? Her eyes ached, threatening to let loose tears she wouldn't be able to stop. He had to be okay. *Had to.*

It occurred to her that she was still wearing her cross body purse and her phone was in it. If she got the chance, she could make a call. It was still on, so she could be located by the GPS.

The car came to a hard stop and she groaned behind her gag. Taynor opened the back door and climbed out. Kelley heard the driver's side door open and then Taynor talking with another man. She looked around her, scanning the car's interior. She tugged against her bonds. They were too tight and she was still too weak to do anything about her predicament. At least for the moment.

Taynor leaned in and roughly dragged Kelley out. She hurt all over from the accident and she felt each cut and bruise as her body hit the hump in the back of the car.

Her eyes watered from the pain, blinding her for a moment when Taynor grabbed a fistful of her hair and jerked her to her feet. He held her up like a marionette as her ankles were bound and she couldn't balance herself.

She blinked the moisture from her eyes and found herself face to face with a man she'd never met. She judged him to be about five-nine, in his early thirties. He had smooth olive skin, a slim mustache, and black hair. He would have been a handsome man if it weren't for the cold calculation in his dark eyes, his expression showing the evil lurking within.

Was he the same man she hadn't been able to see well at Laura's home? The man who had shot Kelley when Taynor shot Laura?

The man swept his gaze down her form then back up to her eyes again. He reached for her and she fought to keep from shrinking back. He reached for her cross body purse and tried to pull it off of her but the strap was too thick and strong and her wrists were tired. He searched the purse and her heart dropped as he took out her cell phone and turned it off. Then he dropped the phone in the dirt and ground it into pieces with his heel.

"Get her and the girl into the truck," he said.

"You've got it, Johnny." Taynor said, and she had no doubt that the man was Johnny Rocha, Taynor's foster brother and one evil sonofabitch. Taynor picked Kelley up and the world spun as he flung her over his shoulder.

She couldn't see where he was headed until he stopped and slung her back down beside a huge refrigerated truck with pictures of Mexican frozen treats. The Spanish words for ice cream and the brand names were written across the side panels. Obviously it was a truck used to import Mexican ice cream treats into the U.S., probably legally.

Her eyes widened. They weren't going to take her in the refrigerated truck, were they? Kelley watched as Taynor went inside and she heard the scrape of metal. While he was out of sight, she watched as Rocha altered his appearance. He looked in the side view mirror of the truck and shaved off not only his mustache but his hair, too, until he was completely bald. She watched as he changed clothes. Like a chameleon, he looked like someone entirely different now.

While Rocha changed the way he looked, Taynor came out and once again threw her over his shoulder, this time carrying her into the truck. It was so cold that goose bumps immediately rose on her skin.

When he set her on her ass again, cold gripped her body, flowing from her legs and ass and up her spine. She saw that three panels had been opened in the truck's floor. She saw Belle lying in one of the openings. The girl was bound and gagged too, her shoes and socks missing. Her eyes were open but foggy looking, like she was dazed.

"You'll be cool in the compartment, but you won't freeze," Taynor said as he picked up Kelley. "I'll be in the third compartment until Johnny gets us across the border."

Fear gripped her body in an iron fist and she struggled, trying to fight, refusing to give up.

Johnny Rocha entered the truck. He looked unrecognizable from the way she'd first seen him. He came up beside Taynor and all the fight went out of Kelley when she saw what he had. Rocha was holding a small syringe filled with a clear fluid.

As Rocha came closer, Kelley started struggling again. But Taynor was almost twice her size and she was bound and helpless. Rocha put the syringe up to her arm and injected her with the fluid.

Almost at once, Kelley's body went limp. All strength left her and she felt relaxed and as if nothing mattered anymore. She wondered vaguely how much she'd been given. For her height and weight it might not take much to keep her down. The thoughts were fleeting and she didn't know that it even mattered.

She didn't struggle as Taynor lowered her into the space next to Belle's. He gave one last satisfied smirk as he moved a piece of the metal flooring over her prison. It fell into place, sealing out all light.

Complete and total darkness, void of sound.

Everything was so quiet that her ears rang from the silence. She shivered from the cold and her teeth would have been chattering if she weren't still wearing a gag. It was like being buried alive, as if she was in a dark coffin six feet below ground.

Panic would have set in but the drug kept her relaxed. She was weak and disoriented from the accident as well as being bound, gagged, in a cold, soundproof space without even a sliver of light stealing inside. And she was drugged.

It didn't take much to keep her breathing slow and even. She struggled against the effects of the drug, but couldn't get up the energy or desire.

Yet a part of her knew she couldn't let her situation get the best of her. She had to overcome the odds and escape from here and save Belle, too.

But then… What did it matter?

She thought of a singsong tune but couldn't hum it with a gag in her mouth.

A thought tried to penetrate her mind. Kelley Petrova would never give up.

Never.

But she couldn't gather the mental energy she needed. She couldn't gather any energy. She could barely think much less act.

Her thoughts turned to Reese and a fist-sized knot formed in her chest even as the drug had her in its hold. Reese had been so still, the side of his face covered in blood. Was he dead?

She prayed to God that he was still alive, that he wasn't hurt. And that he would find her and Belle.

The refrigerated truck started to move. Kelley had the strange sensation of gliding over the ground and being bumped on air currents. The space around her vibrated, and she could only guess they were traveling back down the dirt road now.

In the cramped space and suffocating silence, she had only her thoughts to keep her company. Considering her thoughts were so vague and bounced from one thing to another, that wasn't saying a lot. Her head lolled from side to side as the truck swayed.

A tiny part of her kept trying to pierce the fog of her mind. The practical part. The strong part.

Human traffickers often used drugs to control their victims. Drugging her would keep her from trying to escape. She would be sold and controlled and used however they wanted.

Her eyelids drooped as she rocked in the compartment…and she slowly slipped away.

CHAPTER 16

From a distance, Reese heard voices. His head felt like it was splitting in two and everything felt wrong.

He slowly opened his eyes and found himself flat on his back with Greg Mann, an EMT, crouched next to him. "'Bout time you woke up, McBride," Greg said as he held an oxygen mask up that he had apparently been about to put over Reese's nose and mouth.

Dazed, Reese shoved Greg's hands away. "I don't need that." Despite Greg's attempts to keep him down, Reese pushed himself to a sitting position. He looked around and saw his truck across the street near the jackknifed semi. The truck was upside down, everything crushed and shattered. The street was blocked off and a tow truck was backing up to Reese's obviously totaled vehicle.

"Kelley." Reese tried to scramble to his feet. He made it but stumbled, nearly falling before gaining his bearings. He looked around. "Where's Kelley?"

John came up to stand beside Reese. "Maybe you'd better sit down."

"I'm not sitting down." Reese scowled. "Where the hell is she?"

With a tight expression, John said, "We think she's been kidnapped."

Chills ran down Reese's spine and he struggled to clear his mind as the words sank in. "What the hell are you talking about?"

John gave a nod toward a group of people across the street. "Witnesses saw a man dragging Kelley out of the wreckage and throwing her into the back of a brown sedan. Apparently she tried struggling, but she was hurt. No one has any idea of how badly. The car fled the scene before anyone could stop them."

Reese tried to remain calm. It wasn't going to do him any good to lose it and not get all of the facts. Still, the words lashed out like a whip. "Was it Taynor?"

"The witnesses' descriptions of the man match Taynor's." John looked grim. "Everyone available is out looking for the men who took her and so far they've come up empty."

"Men?" Reese's focus grew clearer. "How many? What did they look like?"

"One other male." John looked at a notebook he was holding. "Late twenties to early thirties, small mustache, olive skin, slender but looks like he might work out."

"I've got to find her." Reese looked around for a vehicle he could commandeer and started toward a black SUV.

"We'll find Kelley." John caught Reese by his upper arm. "You just got knocked out cold in an accident and you shouldn't be driving."

"Fuck that." Reese jerked his arm away from his stepbrother. "I'm not resting until I find her. We're losing time."

"You're not going anywhere, Reese," John said, a hard note in his tone. "You're injured."

Reese narrowed his eyes. "Try and stop me." He strode away for the black SUV.

"Give me a minute." John caught up to Reese and blocked his way. "I'll drive."

Reese thought about telling John to fuck off and get out of his way, but bit back the words.

John gave Reese a hard look and Reese clenched his jaw before he said, "Hurry."

It took only a couple of minutes for John to turn over command of the scene. He got the keys to the black SUV from another detective and he and Reese climbed in.

"According to witnesses, they headed toward I-17." John guided the SUV in that direction. "But like I said, there's been no sign of them."

"You saw the message Zip wrote." Reese gritted his teeth. "They're headed toward the Mexican border in Douglas. We need to get there before they can cross."

"I figured as much, too." John looked at Reese. "That's where we'll go. We'll have to hope that they have no idea Zip could have tipped us off."

They climbed into the vehicle and put on their seatbelts. Lights flashing, John drove the truck away from the scene, rushing through town with the sirens on. He didn't cut the sirens or lights until they reached open road and embarked on the six-hour drive to Douglas.

During the drive, Reese felt like he was going to crawl out of his skin. He and John kept in frequent contact with law enforcement. Every available officer was searching from the air and ground. When it came to a kidnapped officer of the law, the manhunt mobilized all agencies and was even more intense than if it would have been if it were a civilian. Roadblocks had been set up and every vehicle was being stopped and searched.

According to all law enforcement agencies involved, there was no sign of the brown car or anyone matching Taynor's and the other man's descriptions. Nor was anyone seen matching Kelley's description. Reese had no doubt the men had ditched the vehicle and were in another one, and somehow had Kelley hidden.

"For all we know they could be back in Prescott." Reese clenched his fist on his knee. "Hiding out until they think it's safe to go."

"Could be." John adjusted his hands on the steering wheel. "Frankly we could be headed in the wrong direction. For all we know, Taynor went north."

Reese pinched the bridge of his nose with his thumb and forefinger as he thought about it. He raised his head and lowered his hand. "We know that Taynor and Rocha were planning on taking the shipment of women and girls to the Mexican border."

"Although we don't know exactly how they planned to accomplish that without being caught," John said.

"They had to know they'd never get across the border with that semi." Reese considered the problem. "So how could they stash eight females and get them into Mexico?"

John and Reese looked at each other. "Whatever the method was, that could be the way they're taking Belle and Kelley," John said.

"For all we know, they could have planned on taking them in numerous vehicles," Reese said. "But trunks are being opened, backs of trucks searched, and K-9s have been deployed and can detect people who may be stashed somewhere inside the vehicle."

John's grip on the steering wheel tightened. "It's easier smuggling humans into Mexico than out, but security is fairly tight."

Reese considered the problem. "It could be easy to pay off the Mexican customs agents."

"I don't doubt it," John said.

"So it could be one or multiple vehicles." Reese blew out his breath. "We're not any closer to figuring this damned thing out than we were before."

"We'll find her." John looked at Reese. "They won't get away with this."

Reese glanced out the window at the scenery speeding by. No, the bastards wouldn't get away with it. "I'm going to find them one way or another."

"I'm right here with you," John said. "Every damned step of the way. Petrova's like family."

It came out before Reese could stop it. "She's more than family to me."

John gave him a sharp look. "Are you telling me that your relationship has gone beyond work?"

"Yes." Reese pushed his hand through his hair. "Up until recently, we've always had a strictly working relationship. Then things…changed."

"Have you told the captain?" John asked.

Reese shook his head. "Not yet."

John looked back at the road. "Do you plan to anytime soon?"

"We'll pick the right time." Reese nodded. "It'll be soon. After we find Kelley."

"You couldn't have picked a better woman," John said quietly.

Reese didn't need anyone to tell him that fact.

In a way, even though she'd been working by his side for two years, he'd just found her. He wasn't about to lose her now.

* * * * *

Kelley woke with a start and opened her eyes. She was in total darkness. She felt disoriented, confused, and chilled. Her body ached from head to toe and she had a splitting headache. What was going on?

She tried to move but her ankles and wrists were bound and walls pressed in around her, above her, below her. Her heart beat faster and she felt claustrophobic. She recognized the signs of panic as her pulse hiked.

Where was she? What had happened?

Icy chills shot through her as memories started to come to her, one after another. The accident…Reese so still…

And then being kidnapped…drugged…and locked in a compartment at the bottom of a refrigerated truck.

And being taken to Mexico to ultimately be sold to someone in South America.

Sold.

She shuddered, her gut twisting at the thought.

The effects of the drug had faded but she still felt out of it. Still, even through the strands of fog, she knew that she was coming around to herself again. She prayed that it wasn't too late.

Where were she, Belle, and their captors? How close to the border? Had they already crossed?

She swallowed. If they were in Mexico it would be that much harder to escape and get back to the border. She prayed they were still in the U.S.

How much time had passed? Long enough that the effects of the drug were wearing off was all she knew.

Was Reese following? Dear God, he had to have survived the accident and he had to be searching for her. He had seen Zip's note, so he had to be certain that she was being taken to Mexico.

It was all she could do to hold those thoughts in her mind to give her hope.

Kelley started to work at the rope that bound her hands so tightly. The rope cut into her wrists, but they didn't seem to be knotted particularly well. Taynor might not have been the greatest at tying knots or he believed that the effects of the drug would last.

Jaw set, she fought to loosen the rope. She'd start to feel herself drifting and she'd have to force herself to bring her focus back around. Her wrists felt like they were being rubbed raw by the rough rope as she tried to get it off.

The compartment gently rocked her back and forth as she struggled. If she allowed it, the sensation could lull her to asleep again.

Frustration grew inside her until finally she felt a little give in the rope. But it wasn't enough. Her chest ached from fear welling inside her.

The rope slipped a little more and she worked at it all the harder. Moments later, the rope slid off her wrists.

She hurried to take off the gag and then let out a rush of air. As she did, she realized that she'd never had a problem breathing in the cramped space. She'd been too out of it to care when she'd first been put into the compartment.

What if she called to Belle? Would the girl hear her? Or would she risk being heard by Taynor and Rocha? Then she remembered that Taynor had planned to climb into a compartment himself to avoid being caught.

No, she couldn't risk calling out.

Wriggling and squirming, she tried reached for her ankles in the cramped space. She'd been put into a small compartment, and even though she was petite, there wasn't a lot of room to bend. It took a while but with one hand she finally reached the rope that so tightly bound her ankles. It didn't take her as long to undo the knot around her ankles as it had for her wrists.

She placed her palms on the metal plate that was currently her ceiling in the refrigerated section of the truck's floor. It was smooth, with no seams that she could find. Of course the seams were there. She just couldn't feel them.

Using her hands and knees, she tried pushing up against her ceiling, but it wouldn't budge, not even a fraction.

Anger started a slow burn in her chest. She'd tried desperately not to fall prey to her emotions, but it was all becoming too much. The compartment felt like it was closing in on her and soon she would be unable to breathe. Her rational mind knew that the air supply would probably be just fine, but she couldn't push away that niggling fear.

The silence around her was so complete that her ears rang with it. She was in a soundproof insulated space. She wondered if the truck also had something to mask odor that was strong enough to keep K-9s from smelling humans. But then they were probably not as worried about humans being smuggled into Mexico from the United States as opposed to smuggling from Mexico into the U.S.

Although, it was possible that this same truck was used to smuggle Mexican Nationals into the U.S., and then traffic U.S. citizens into Mexico.

The drug had worn off considerably more and she was becoming more aware of the pain in her head from the accident and every ache in her body. Her shoulder, where she'd been shot, felt like it had been wrenched somewhere along the way.

She let out her breath, trying to decide what to attempt next when the swaying of the compartment stopped. She was certain the vehicle had come to a halt.

Her breathing came faster and she prayed someone had found her.

CHAPTER 17

Reese felt like slamming his fist into a brick wall. As wound up as he was, he could probably do some serious damage to a wall, not to mention his fist. His head ached from the injury sustained in the accident and more than likely it ached from frustration, too. He didn't have any water so he dry-swallowed a couple of Tylenol that he found in a bottle in the glove compartment.

John glanced from the road to look at Reese. "It could be they're still in Prescott."

"My gut tells me they're on their way to the border by now." Reese's entire body was so tense that he felt like his control would snap. "We've got to find them before they cross."

As John drove, Reese tried to work everything over in his mind. During the trip down to the southern part of the state, Reese had called in every favor he could think of, making contact with his sources and pressing them for information.

So far nothing. Not a damned thing.

The first person he'd called was his brother, Garrett. As a private investigator, Garrett had his own sources and unconventional ways of finding information, ways that weren't as readily available to the police department. Garrett also had methods of making his sources talk that Reese couldn't legally use. Reese was holding out hope that Garrett would come up with something.

"We're going to have to make a quick stop for fuel. We're running on empty." John broke into Reese's thoughts as he pulled the SUV off the highway onto the Benson exit they needed to take to get to Douglas. He drove into a gas station that was across from a McDonald's. "Tell you what. You gas up the SUV and I'll run across the street and grab us a couple of Big Macs, fries, and drinks."

Reese wanted to argue that they didn't have time to stop for any reason. But there was no arguing that they weren't going to get anywhere if they didn't stop for gas. And they wouldn't be at peak performance if they didn't fuel their bodies, too.

"Make mine a double bacon cheeseburger with a large Dr. Pepper and large fries," Reese said as John started to climb out. "Two of the burgers."

"You've got it." John gave a nod before jogging across the street.

Filling the SUV's large fuel tank took some time, and Reese's body ached with the need for action. He dragged his palm down his face as he waited, his patience waning. He winced when his hand rubbed over a large laceration on his temple. In the rush to find Kelley, he hadn't allowed himself to dwell on injuries he had sustained from the accident.

Fact was that his entire body ached, including his hand with the missing fingers. The ghost pains were almost as bad as all of his new injuries. At least he hadn't fractured anything in the accident—not that he knew of.

Benson was a good seventy miles from Douglas and the Mexican border and there was still no sign of the bastards who'd taken Kelley. Hell, law enforcement agencies still had no idea what kind of vehicle Taynor and Rocha were in.

In his gut, Reese was sure that they were headed in the right direction. They just needed a break. He wondered, not for the first time, if Belle was being smuggled with Kelley.

Finally the SUV's tank was full. John returned, carrying two white McDonald's bags and two large drinks just as Reese took the receipt from the pump.

Reese stood by the driver's side door as he tucked the receipt into his wallet. "I'll drive."

John shook his head as he handed Reese one of the fast food bags and a drink. "I've already made it clear to you. You were knocked out, which means you've got a concussion and you're not driving. Personally, I'd like to reach our destination. Alive."

With a scowl, Reese took the bag and headed to the passenger side of the SUV. He didn't like the feeling of being out of control with any of this one damned bit. Driving always made him feel more in control than sitting in the passenger seat letting someone else have the wheel.

They climbed into the SUV. After Reese strapped in, he dug into his bag and pulled out one of the bacon cheeseburgers. He unwrapped it and took a big bite. He chewed and swallowed, and realized that John had been right about getting some food into him. He hadn't had anything since breakfast, at least eight hours ago.

Reese managed to get both cheeseburgers and all of his fries down as he made more calls. Somewhere they had to get a break.

When they were fifteen miles from Douglas and the Mexican border, they were no closer to figuring out where Kelley was and what kind of vehicle she might have been smuggled in.

John glanced from the road to Reese. "Where do you want to start first?" John asked before looking at the road again.

Reese dragged his hand down his face. "Head to the border. One of our contacts has got to call with information that will help us find Rocha and Kelley."

John guided the SUV toward the Mexican border. "You never know, we might see something suspicious while we keep an eye out."

With a nod, Reese said, "That's what I'm counting on."

* * * * *

In case Rocha or Taynor was coming to check on her, Kelley hurried to tie the gag around her head and slipped the ropes onto her wrists. It was so cramped in the compartment that she could barely get the gag tied and ropes back on her wrists. She didn't have time to put the ropes over her ankles.

Metal scraped metal as the lid of the compartment started to slide away. Light and chilled air rushed in along with the sound of the motor running. Kelley closed her eyes and let her head loll to the side to make it appear as though she was still drugged and out cold.

"Should we give her another shot?" Taynor said aloud and Kelley had to keep herself from reacting. No, damn it. No more shots.

"Nah." Rocha's voice. "Getting low on the shit we drugged her with. We'd have to use something different. We'll have her across the border in twenty minutes and she'll still be too drugged to do anything. We don't want to give her too much."

Kelley felt a small measure of relief. They weren't across the border yet and they weren't going to give her another shot.

"I think we should just kill the bitch." Taynor spoke in a harsh growl. "After what she's done—"

"I haven't forgotten," Rocha said with a hard edge to his words. "When we deliver her to the buyer, she'll pay. She'll be nothing but a whore to whoever wants to fuck her." Rocha gave a harsh laugh. "The buyer likes to loan out his whores and he's going to like this one. We *will* see the bitch pay. It will be worse for her than killing her."

Kelley's entire body started to tighten and she had to fight to keep any expression off her face and to look relaxed from the drugs.

A phone rang and Kelley heard Rocha answer, "What?" Silence as Rocha listened. "How the fuck did they find out?" he said after a moment. Another pause. "Shit."

"What's wrong?" Taynor asked.

"One of my men told me that fucker, Zip, left a note after I blew a hole in his gut," Rocha said. "The message told the cops we're headed for the border."

"Shit," Taynor said.

"They'll be waiting for us," Rocha said with fury in his voice.

"Cops don't know what we're driving," Taynor said.

Rocha let out a sound like a growl. "Unless Zip told them."

"I don't think Zip knew," Taynor said.

"He knew." Rocha practically spat the words. "It was one of the reasons why I shut him up permanently, before he spilled anything else to the cops. Should have shot him in the head."

"What are we going to do?" Taynor sounded panicked now.

"I've got to think about it," Rocha said. "We'll stay here until I've got this figured out."

"What about the detective?" A derisive note was in Taynor's words when he said *detective*.

"We'll have to shoot her up before she wakes," Rocha said. "What I've got will keep the bitch out until morning."

Kelley kept still. If they tried to drug her now, she'd have to make a move. She couldn't let them shoot her up again.

"What the hell?" Taynor's voice grew closer to Kelley. "Her wrists weren't tied like that when I left her. Something's different."

"You're probably imagining things." Rocha dismissed Taynor's words. "Move out of my way. We'll give her a shot then seal her up again and get going."

"Just a second." Taynor's voice was closer now. "Her ankles aren't tied anymore. I know I—"

Kelley reacted automatically. She opened her eyes, grabbed Taynor's head, and jerked him down at the same time she rammed her knee up and to his nose.

Taynor screamed in shock and pain. Kelley lunged for a gun that was in the front of his pants. She wrapped her hand around the grip and started to pull it out when she felt the hard press of a barrel against her temple.

Her skin went cold and she froze. "Hold up your hands and move away from Taynor," Rocha said with fury in his voice.

She leaned back, her hands up, her body stiff. Adrenaline pumped through her, masking the pain from her injuries. All she felt was the pounding of her heart and heard the blood rushing in her ears, her body wired from the adrenaline.

Taynor regained his balance and slowly brought his gaze to Kelley, blood gushing from his nose. He raised his arm and backhanded her so hard it threw her backward, against the side of the compartment she'd been kneeling in.

"Shoot her up," Taynor said, blood flowing over his lips.

"Told you I'm running low," Rocha said. "We'll have to shut her up another way."

Taynor grabbed her by her hair and jerked her to her feet. Pain shot through her scalp where she'd sustained more injuries in the accident. He dragged her out of the compartment then threw her to the floor of the truck.

She only had a moment to see him bringing the grip of his pistol down hard on her, slamming it into the side of her head.

Everything went black.

* * * * *

Parked in the SUV with John on the Arizona side of the border, Reese narrowed his eyes as he watched vehicles pass through from Douglas into Agua Prieta, Mexico. The Mexican customs agents gave a good show of checking each vehicle with more diligence than normal. Reese was afraid it was just that— all show. They could have been paid off. Rocha could already be across the border with Kelley.

They'd provided the Mexican Customs agents with a photograph of Taynor and a rendering of Rocha's image. No photographs were on file for Rocha, aka Johnny Rocket, so the only thing they had to go by was the sketch.

Reese's phone rang. He saw by the caller ID that it was his brother, Garrett. Reese pressed the ON button and raised the phone to his ear. "What have you got?" Reese said as way of an answer.

"Just met up with one of Fat T's boys," Garrett said. "They call him Junior because he's a smaller version of Fat T."

"I've heard of him." Reese straightened in his seat and just about knocked over the rest of his large Dr. Pepper from the drink holder. "What can you tell me?"

"It took some convincing, but I think I've got something you can use," Garrett said and Reese had a feeling that Garrett hadn't used conventional methods of interrogation. "Junior said that he saw a big silver truck one time when he was with Fat T and Johnny Rocha. Thinks it might have been an ice cream truck because it had pictures of ice cream treats on it."

"An ice cream truck?" Reese frowned, thinking out loud.

"Not a typical ice cream truck that goes around a neighborhood. Most likely a large refrigerated truck of some sort," Garrett said. "Maybe one that isn't really refrigerated or has some kind of hidden compartments insulated against the cold to smuggle humans."

Reese's mind raced. "Mexico exports frozen treat items to parts of the U.S., including Arizona. That would be a perfect front to smuggle humans out of the U.S. when the truck returns to Mexico."

"Sounds like a good possibility to me," Garrett said.

"Thanks, bro." Reese blew out his breath in a rush. "We're at the border but haven't seen any kind of refrigerated truck. I'll call it in now." He cut the connection and glanced at John as he grabbed the radio. "If they haven't already crossed the border, we have a good lead on Rocha and Taynor."

Reese's heart rate increased as he spoke into the radio, giving the new information to be relayed to all law enforcement agencies and Mexican Customs.

Reese looked back at the border. In the long line of cars waiting to cross into Mexico, there was no big ice cream truck, or refrigerated truck of any kind.

They got out of the SUV and headed for the border station and walked up to the Mexican Customs Agents. John spoke fluent Spanish, leaning toward Spanglish in this case, which included Mexican slang spoken in states along the border. John explained the situation to the agents and asked if they had let a refrigerated truck of any kind pass by earlier today.

Reese's Spanish wasn't fluent, but he understood enough to know what John was asking the agents. The agents said a refrigerated truck had gone through earlier but it had not been a truck that delivered ice cream. It had been a truck filled with frozen meats from the U.S.

"Doesn't mean it wasn't them," Reese said as he and John walked away from the border and back toward the SUV. His mouth was in a hard, tight line. "But if it was, it means we're too late."

John nodded. "I hope to hell that's not the case."

Reese clenched his hands into fists as they reached the SUV. "For all we know the Mexican border agents were paid off to keep quiet about the truck crossing the border. Wouldn't be the first time, I'm sure."

"We'll stay put for now and keep an eye out," John said. "Could be we beat Rocha and Taynor here."

Reese stared at the border crossing. It went against his grain to do nothing. But right now all they could do was wait and pray for the best.

Chapter 18

Kelley groaned as she stirred. She tried to roll over but found herself confined in a tight space. She grimaced as her head throbbed and opened her eyes to total and complete darkness. Memories flowed back to her. She was in the refrigerated truck in the hidden compartment and she'd been knocked out once again, this time by the butt of Taynor's handgun. Surprisingly, they hadn't bound her again.

How much time had passed? Were they across the border now?

The thought made panic rise up inside her like a flock of birds in her chest. She inhaled slowly and blew her breath out before breathing in again. Her deep, even inhalations and exhalations helped to calm her.

Whatever happened, there was no way they'd be able to keep her captive.

A chill rolled over her, causing goose bumps to rise on her skin. Tactics used by human traffickers ranged from death threats to promises of retribution on family members and friends. Drugs were a big part of it, and that part did make her heart thump harder again and her stomach to churn. If she were to be drugged, there would be no way to fight back, no way to extricate herself from the horrors of being a sex slave. She'd have to do it in any moments of lucidity she might have.

The churning in her stomach grew worse. She was fortunate that neither Rocha nor Taynor had attempted to rape her. She'd be able to tell if they had while she was drugged, and she was positive they hadn't.

She began to feel an urgent need to pee and she gritted her teeth. Time seemed to drag on as she pushed up against her ceiling, trying to open the compartment. She heard a scraping noise and then the metal panel that served as her ceiling began to move. Thoughts about taking on her captors again went through her mind, but she was still too dizzy and not in a good position to do anything. Yet.

When the metal panel was moved aside, she looked up to see the muzzle of a pistol trained on her by Rocha. She winced from the harsh sound that throbbed through her aching head when Taynor dropped the panel he'd just moved aside.

"Out." Rocha motioned with the gun for her to climb out of the compartment.

Her throat grew dry and her heart pounded harder as she obeyed him. When she stood on the floor of the refrigerated truck she shivered. He motioned for her to go to the truck's open rear doors.

As she walked toward the back of the truck, she blinked her eyes. It was dark but she could see that they were in an old building, a barn from the looks of it. Silvery moonlight spilled in through gaps in the weathered boards.

"Where are we?" she asked.

"Shut up." Taynor growled the words.

"I have to use the bathroom." She looked at Rocha. "Please."

Rocha waved his gun. "Climb down."

She wobbled a little as she stepped onto the bumper, still weak from one thing after another that had happened. She wasn't sure if it had been stupid to try and take on Taynor and Rocha earlier. In her desperation to escape before they crossed the border it had been all she could think to do.

Rocha grabbed her upper arm as she reached the back of the truck and dragged her down. She stumbled and would have fallen if he didn't have a hold on her.

When they were on the straw-covered dirt floor of the building, she realized that the truck was in a large old barn with what looked like loose boards in the walls, the boards gray and splintered. Stalls ran the length of the building, a couple with doors hanging off their hinges.

As she scanned the barn, she saw eight-year-old Belle hunching over in front of an old straw bale, her knees up against her chest and her arms around her shins, her feet bare. A measure of relief went through Kelley to see that Belle was alive and on the surface appeared safe and sound—as sound as she could be after seeing her mother murdered in front of her and being kidnapped.

Rocha waved his weapon in the direction of the back of the barn. "Do your thing over there, Detective, where we can watch you."

"Not outside?" she asked.

"Either shut up and do as you're told or piss your pants," Rocha said.

She'd had to do a lot of humiliating things over the course of her career in law enforcement, and right now she had to go too badly to be embarrassed or to argue. She raised her chin and avoided Rocha's and Taynor's eyes as they followed her to the back of the barn. As she pushed down her jeans she realized she was still wearing her purse.

The night was starting to cool and she shivered in the near darkness and took care of business in the rear of the barn. When she finished, she straightened, her body aching from all it had been through as she zipped and buttoned her jeans.

"Sit by the girl." Taynor nodded toward the straw bale where Belle was.

Kelley obeyed and sat close to Belle. Her mind raced as she took in her barely lit surroundings, calculating her chances of escaping to get help. She could be in either Arizona or Mexico for all she knew. There were too many things working against her right now for her to try to escape, including her lack of knowledge of the territory she was in, her injuries, and the fact she couldn't take off and leave without Belle.

"Don't think of leaving," Rocha said in a deadly tone, as if he could read her mind. "We'll kill the girl if you try to escape. Understand?"

Kelley's throat worked. "Yes," she said.

The men moved away, speaking in low tones. Kelley tried to listen but they were speaking too quietly for her to hear.

She turned to Belle who looked terrified. "Hi, Belle, honey. Have they hurt you?"

Belle shook her head but didn't speak.

Kelley put her arm around Belle's shoulders and felt the girl tremble. She stroked Belle's tangled hair away from her face, wishing there was some way to comfort her. Kelley thought about the times her mother would comfort her by brushing her hair out until it shone.

She reached into her cross body purse and dug out her small hairbrush. As she did so, she glanced at Taynor and Rocha and saw them still deep in conversation. She shifted and began brushing the girl's hair, untangling the long blonde strands. "You're so brave, Belle."

The girl's trembling gradually stopped and with her big blue eyes she looked at Kelley. "I'm not brave." Belle's voice shook and tears glistened in her eyes. "I miss my mom."

"I know, honey." Kelley continued to brush Belle's hair. She lowered her voice. "I will get us out of here."

Belle nodded but said nothing.

"Did you hear them say where we are?" Kelley asked quietly. "Did they say if they've crossed the border into Mexico?"

Belle shook her head. "One of them talked to somebody on the phone and said we'll be crossing the border into Mexico tomorrow."

Kelley let out a breath. "Did you hear anything else?"

With a frown, Belle looked deep in thought. "I don't think they're going to put us in the truck again. They're going to find another way to take us into Mexico."

As Kelley turned that over in her mind, she wondered what the men were now planning. She was pretty sure that the ice cream truck had been a way that Rocha could have taken them over undetected. But if Rocha and Taynor believed their method of smuggling had been compromised, they now needed to find another way. That thought gave her hope.

Belle caught Kelley's attention as she added, "They talked about paying someone to help them get across."

Kelley looked at the girl, her stomach dropping. "Rocha and Taynor talked about paying off a Mexican customs agent?"

With a nod, Belle said, "Yes. I remember them saying they would pay off as many agents as it took."

Damn. Kelley didn't speak her thought aloud. She didn't want Belle to know she was worried.

"People are looking for us," Kelley said. "My partner will find us."

With those words, Kelley's heart lurched. She didn't know for sure that Reese had survived the accident. Yet somehow she felt with certainty that Reese was alive and searching for her. She didn't know how she could feel so confident, but she did. It was better than the alternative—being afraid that Reese was dead…and that no one was coming for her and Belle.

"What are you doing?" Rocha's voice cut into Kelley's thoughts.

She jerked her attention to the man who had his eyes narrowed. "I'm brushing Belle's hair. It's calming her down."

Rocha studied her for a long moment. "What else do you have in that purse?"

"You searched it." Kelley didn't look away from him. "You know all I have is the brush and my ID."

The man held out his hand. "Give it to me." She held out the brush but he shook his head. "The purse," he said.

She set the brush on the ground then shifted and took off the purse. She was surprised he hadn't asked her for it earlier.

When she held it out, he snatched it from her grasp. He dug through it again. He pulled out a tissue, two pens, and her checkbook. Lastly he brought out her wallet, which also contained her credentials, including her badge.

He flipped it open and scanned it. With a smirk he tossed the wallet aside so that it landed in the dirt. "You won't be needing that anymore."

She tried to school her expression. It wouldn't do her any good to be antagonistic with him. Not after what she'd already tried and the fact that he could drug her again. She needed to stay lucid if she was going to save herself and Belle.

Rocha sneered and threw her purse in the opposite direction along with the lipstick, tissue, and pen.

When Rocha was looking away, Belle put her hand on Kelley's arm. She leaned in close and Kelley lowered her head so that she could hear what Belle had to say.

"I have my phone in my pocket," the girl said quietly.

Kelley's eyes widened and she drew away from Belle. "You have a phone?" she whispered.

The girl nodded. "They've always had my hands tied until now, so I couldn't get it. I was going to dial 9-1-1 like Mom told me to if anything happened. I was afraid they would find it."

"Let's wait for the right time and then I'll call for help," Kelley whispered.

Belle nodded again. "I knew you would save me when I saw you."

Kelley studied Belle. How could the girl believe in Kelley when her mom had been killed in front of her and Kelley had passed out? Wasn't it her fault that the girl's mother was dead?

Before Kelley could say anything else, she saw Rocha approaching them. For a moment she was afraid that he'd overheard. But instead he tossed a bag at her and Belle.

Kelley let it drop in front of them. Cautiously, she looked into the plastic bag. Inside was a Slim Jim, a small bag of Doritos, a package of M&Ms, and a single powdered donut that was loose in the plastic grocery bag. Kelley's stomach growled, even at the sight of the pitiful fare.

Kelley ignored Rocha and looked from the meager stash to Belle. "Are you hungry, Belle?"

The girl's shoulders rose and fell in a shrug.

"You should eat something even if you don't feel hungry." Kelley opened the Slim Jim, the orange grease glistening in the package. "You need it to help give you energy." She tore the Slim Jim and handed half to Belle. "Here. Eat this."

Belle frowned but took it. She tentatively bit into the meat then grimaced. "It's awful."

Kelley managed a smile. "It's greasy but it will give you a little protein."

The girl was still frowning as she took another bite, but she finished it off. Ignoring Rocha and Taynor, Kelley and Belle ate the Doritos and donut, then opened up the package of M&Ms. They ate the candies one at a time, making them last. Kelley made sure the girl had most of their meager supply of food.

When they finished eating, Belle's eyelids drooped. Kelley put her arm around the girl's shoulders and brought her close so that her head rested on Kelley's chest. She gently rocked Belle until the girl's lips parted and her breathing came deep and even.

Likely Belle had the phone in one of her front pockets. Kelley wanted to get it from her, but now wasn't the time. She needed to get the phone from Belle when Taynor and Rocha were nowhere around.

Even though she was exhausted and beat up from everything that had happened that day, Kelley was wide-awake. She watched Taynor and Rocha as they talked. Rocha was clearly a leader who was used to things going his way. He had a constant nasty and ferocious expression. Taynor was obviously intimidated and looked like he was attempting to walk on eggshells with everything he did or said.

Rocha's phone rang and he answered, barking out the words. "Give me some good news." He listened to whoever was on the other end. The scowl on his face faded to be replaced by a smile of satisfaction. "Good," Rocha finally said. "Bring it to me."

He walked away from Kelley until she could no longer hear what Rocha was saying. She had a feeling he was giving directions and didn't want Kelley to hear.

After he disconnected the call, Rocha shoved the phone into his pocket. "Darrell," Rocha called out and Taynor reappeared. Rocha inclined his head to Kelley and Belle. "Tie them up and do a better job this time."

Taynor and Rocha walked toward Kelley and Belle. Kelley gently shook Belle. "Wake up, honey," she said right before Taynor grabbed Kelley by her upper arm and jerked her to her feet.

He practically dragged her toward a support beam. Several feet away she saw an old pickaxe. Could she get to it and use it to get away with Belle from Taynor and Rocha?

Taynor shoved her down next to the support beam with such force that she landed hard on her tailbone and jarred her head against the beam. She had the fleeting thought that when this was all over she really did need a vacation.

I will escape, she said fiercely in her mind. *With Belle...and we'll both be safe.*

Rocha dragged a sobbing Belle to the support beam and then Taynor was tying Kelley and Belle back-to-back with the beam between them.

Eventually, Kelley pretended to fall asleep while the men spoke to each other. Or rather, while Rocha did all the talking. For a long time she watched them from beneath her lashes. She thought again of the pick and wondered if she could get it whenever the men fell asleep. But it would be unwieldy and the men had at least one handgun.

Most of the time Rocha spoke too quietly for her to hear anything. Every now and then, he would go on a rant, raging about the men who had snitched on him, and who he was going to have killed once he was in Mexico. He planned on sending an assassin to do his dirty work. Apparently he wasn't planning on returning to the States for a while, choosing to remain hidden in Mexico until the dust settled.

While the men thought she was sleeping, Kelley worked at the rope around her wrists that were tied behind her. When Taynor had bound her, she'd done her best to push her arms outward so that the rope would be at least a little loose when he finished. However, he had tied it so tightly that having any slack was impossible and the rope was nearly cutting off her circulation.

Still, Kelley worked at the rope, ceaselessly trying to remove it. Her wrists had already been rubbed raw from her earlier efforts and her eyes watered as the pain turned into a fiery burn. She was certain they were bleeding by now. Gradually her body numbed from the pain. She was exhausted and her head pounded, but she couldn't give up.

With her head still bowed as if in sleep, Kelley kept an eye on Rocha and Taynor. Eventually they fell silent and she saw that they had fallen asleep. Taynor was on the ground and leaning up against one of the truck's tires, his head to the side and his mouth open as he snored. Rocha was sitting on the ground, too, his back to a hay bale, his arms folded and his chin resting on his chest.

Kelley was nearly overcome with exhaustion but she couldn't give up. *Wouldn't* give up. As the rope started to give, new life flooded into her. She glanced again at the pickaxe. She was so exhausted, her aches and pains screaming, that she didn't know if she could wield it well enough to save herself and Belle.

She felt Belle stir as her elbow brushed Kelley's. "Belle," Kelley whispered. "Are you awake?"

"Yes." The girl sounded sleepy.

Kelley was nearly out of the rope, adrenaline making her heart beat faster. "Which of your pockets is the phone in?"

"My front pocket," the girl said. "The left one. But I can't get it 'cause my hands are tied."

"I'm going to put my hand in your pocket in a moment and take it." The rope slid off Kelley's wrists as she spoke. "Then I'm calling my partner."

"Okay," Belle said.

With her eyes still on Taynor and Rocha, Kelley scooted a few inches to her right, Belle's left. She reached around the support beam, groping for Belle and finally touching her leg. She moved her fingers up until she felt the lump in Belle's pocket. She found the opening to the pocket and eased her fingers inside until she touched the cool, hard shell of the phone.

In moments, Kelley had her hand wrapped around the device and brought it up to her side. She opened the flip phone and keyed in Reese's cell number as she continued to glance at the two men.

She heard a faint ring and brought the phone to her ear, praying that Reese was alive.

CHAPTER 19

Reese and John maintained their vigil at the border, watching every vehicle that passed by. Many trucks had crossed the line but none that were refrigerated. Every time a truck approached the border, Reese had to hold back from going to the Mexican agents and demanding to search every vehicle himself. It wouldn't do any good—the agents had already refused his help.

Darkness closed in and Reese dragged his hand down his face. His entire body ached from being wound so tightly. The accident had a hand in the aches and pains he felt, but for the most part he ignored it all. His thoughts were focused on Kelley.

John stared out the window as a rusted Blazer with a broken taillight approached the border.

Reese's phone rang. He picked it up off the seat, glanced at the caller ID, and saw a number he didn't recognize.

"Detective McBride," he answered and heard the tiredness and frustration in his own voice.

"Reese." An urgent whisper came over the phone and his heart jerked as he realized it was Kelley.

"Kelley." Reese straightened in his seat and glanced at John whose attention had swiveled to him. "Are you all right, honey? Where are you?"

"I don't know where we are." Her voice sounded tight. "But if Belle heard correctly, we're still in Arizona, near the Mexico border."

"Thank God." Reese gripped his phone so tightly that his knuckles ached. "How did you get hold of a phone?"

"It's Belle's. Rocha and Taynor obviously didn't think to check her pockets," Kelley whispered. "Can't talk long. The battery is low and Rocha and Taynor are close."

"Are you in a refrigerated truck?" Reese asked.

"We were in hidden compartments in the floor of a truck that transports ice cream from Mexico into Arizona," she said. "They're going to switch to something else. I don't know what, yet."

"What can you tell me about where you are right now?" he asked urgently.

"We're in a barn, so the truck is hidden," she said. "I'm pretty sure this place is abandoned because the barn looks like it's falling apart."

"They're in an abandoned barn," Reese said to John who grabbed the radio and started relaying the information.

An edge of fear that he'd never heard in Kelley's voice accompanied her inner strength as she continued, "Just in case… there's something I want to tell you."

"We're going to find you." He heard the ferocity in his words as he interrupted her, not wanting her to consider defeat in any way.

"I love you, Reese." She sounded choked up as she spoke. "I think I always have."

It struck him like a punch to his heart, as if he might never see her again. He refused to believe it or let it happen. "I love you, Kelley. I *will* find you."

The line went silent.

"Kelley?" he nearly shouted her name. *"Kelley."*

The phone beeped in his ear, telling him the call had been disconnected.

"Shit." His mind raced. Had she been caught on the phone or had she severed the connection because Rocha or Taynor had come near her? The battery could even have gone dead.

Her words repeated in his mind over and over. *"I love you, Reese."*

"They're somewhere here in the valley," he said to John. "Now that we know Kelley and Belle are here, we'll be able to get the local police to set up road blocks before any vehicles can get close to the border."

"It's not going to be easy finding the barn with it being so dark out," John said. "Not to mention we have no idea how close or how far away they may be."

Reese gave a grim nod. He and John spent the next fifteen minutes contacting sources and making plans.

As soon as it was arranged, they drove to the U.S. Customs and Border Protection airfield where they parked so that they could board a helicopter to search for possible locations where Rocha and Taynor could be holding Kelley and Belle.

The whir of the helicopter's rotors was nearly deafening as Reese and John kept their heads down and hurried to the copter.

They boarded and were given headphones to cut out the roar and to allow communication between Reese, John, and the two Border Patrol agents who were with them, one of whom was the pilot. The pilot was Ben Holloway and the other Border Patrol agent was Jorge Munoz.

It had been some time since Reese had been in a helicopter, and he'd never been too crazy about flying in them. He had a swooping sensation in his gut as they lifted from the pad and took off, but his mind was solely focused on Kelley and finding her. Little else mattered.

The helicopter's searchlight swept over the ground as they covered territory around Douglas. Most of the locations with barns big enough to house a refrigerated truck had occupied homes on the property, the barns seeming to be in good repair. According to Kelley, the barn that they were in was in poor condition.

The area was so large that there was a lot of territory to cover. The longer it took, the tighter Reese's gut seemed to twist and the harder he clenched his jaws and his fists. He had to rein in his emotions if he was going to keep a clear head.

All four of them peered out into the night, searching… searching. It was so damned dark.

Some time later, Agent Munoz said, "I think I've found something." He gestured to the east. "Right there."

Agent Holloway did a flyby, and Reese's throat grew tight as he looked at the dark barn that Agent Munoz pointed out. It was hard to tell in the darkness, but it looked weathered and dilapidated. A house was close to the barn, but with its weed-choked yard, the front door hanging by its hinges, and the roof that was caved in on the west side, it was no doubt abandoned.

Munoz called it in before looking over his shoulder at Reese. "Border Patrol and the sheriff's department are on their way."

Holloway circled the barn and house. Reese saw no activity and the barn was dark, not even the slightest glow peeking through the boards. If Taynor and Rocha were holding Belle and Kelley in this barn, they must have had all lights off.

The barn was so far from Douglas that it took twenty minutes for the Border Patrol to arrive, followed by the sheriff's department. Reese had never taken his eyes off of the barn, so he was certain that if their quarry was there, they hadn't left.

When their backup arrived, Holloway lowered the helicopter so that it hovered a few feet above the ground, the wind from the rotors stirring dust and grass. Reese, John, and Munoz jumped out of the copter while Holloway guided the craft into the air again and circled the barn, the searchlight illuminating the barn.

John, Reese, and Munoz joined the Border Patrol agents, the sheriff, and his deputies. The Border Patrol agents had two German shepherds trained to detect humans and drugs.

Reese was a long way from his own jurisdiction so as much as he wanted to take charge he had to let the sheriff be in control.

Sheriff Pike appeared to be a good man who was serious and determined to rescue Kelley and the girl. He broke the agents and deputies into teams to cover the back and front. Reese and John were with Agent Munoz and Deputy Carlyle and would enter from the front of the barn. Reese would take the lead on his team.

Bulletproof vests were distributed and strapped on and they came up with two extra for Reese and John.

The night was cool and quiet, the silence broken only by a pack of coyotes yipping in the distance. Stars sparkled overhead in a glittering swathe across the dark sky, and the moon was silvery and bright.

John and Reese moved to one side of the huge barn doors while Munoz and Carlyle took the other side. Like the other men, Reese held his weapon in a two-handed grip, ready for anything that might greet them from inside the barn.

Reese waited for the signal that everyone was in place. Reese shouted "Police!" as the doors were shoved open. At the same time, the team from the backside of the barn broke in, also with shouts of "Police!"

Nothing was inside the barn.

No truck, no men, no Kelley, no Belle. There was no sign that anyone had been here for years.

Reese felt like he'd been punched to the gut. Where were Kelley and Belle? The men worked their way through the barn, checking the hayloft as well as the stalls.

Nothing.

Reese dragged his hand down his face. He cursed beneath his breath and turned to John.

"I was so damned sure they were here." Reese holstered his Glock. *"Damn it,"* he growled.

John rested his hand on Reese's shoulder. "We'll find them."

Resisting shrugging off John's hand, Reese took a deep breath, trying to calm himself. "We'll just keep looking."

"You should get some rest." John removed his hand from Reese's shoulder and glanced at the time on his phone. "It's closing in on two a.m."

"I don't have time." Reese started out of the barn. "They could be heading across the border even as we speak."

John nodded. "Then we'd better get to searching."

Reese's phone vibrated in its holster. He always kept it on vibrate when necessary, during times like this. He pulled the phone out of his pocket to see that he had a text message and went to his message screen. His heart squeezed when he saw that the phone number on the text was the one Kelley had called him from earlier.

He clicked on the message and read it.

> *They're getting ready to move us. An hour ago Rocha saw a searchlight and it spooked him. Don't know where we're being taken.*

Reese read through the message twice then handed his phone to John who scanned it.

When John looked up, he said, "They must have been in one of the other barns that we passed before coming to this one."

"My thoughts exactly. We've got to get to them before they move out." Reese turned and jogged to where Sheriff Pike was talking with a couple of his deputies.

Reese explained about the text. Pike nodded. "We'll be ready when you locate the next target."

After Reese caught up with Agent Munoz, John joined them and they hurried to the helicopter where Holloway had found a place to land in a grassy field. They ducked beneath the rotors and climbed into the craft.

As the helicopter rose, Reese prayed they would find the location where Kelley and Belle were and soon.

* * * * *

Rocha started the big truck and turned the headlights on, nearly blinding Kelley. Kelley had just shoved the phone into her front pocket and she prayed he hadn't seen her. Rocha climbed out of the truck, his newly shaved head gleaming in the headlights.

Taynor approached Rocha. "What now?"

"Get the bitch and the girl into the back." Rocha gave a nod in the direction of the refrigerated truck. "We gotta get the fuck out of here before that helicopter comes back."

Kelley glanced at the pick again. Could she get to it before Taynor got to her? No, she didn't have enough time. She set her jaw as Taynor came toward her to take the bindings off of her wrists. When he saw that her wrists were already untied, he narrowed his gaze. With a furious expression, he swung his foot, and kicked her in the side with his boot.

She cried out, nearly doubling over as pain shot through her side and her chest. He'd kicked her so hard she briefly wondered if he'd cracked one of her ribs.

"I'll teach you to get out of your fucking ropes." He swung his foot back again but Kelley managed to roll out of his way.

"They fell off." She scrambled away, her eyes watering and her body screaming from the pain. "I could have left, but I stayed."

"Get the bitch into the truck like I told you," Rocha shouted. "Now."

Taynor walked over to Kelley, grabbed her by her hair and jerked her to her feet. Stars burst in her mind and she felt momentarily dizzy as it felt like fire seared her lacerated scalp.

Warm blood trickled down the side of her face as the head wound reopened.

He pushed her away from him and she stumbled out of the glow of headlights, every ache in her body seeming to come alive. Her mind once again clouded from pain and she had to struggle to remain upright.

This sonofabitch was going to pay as soon as she had the opportunity. Rocha had woken when Kelley had been on the phone with Reese and she'd barely been able to put the phone away before he looked over at her. He'd kicked Taynor's thigh, forcing him awake.

Later, when Rocha was ranting about the helicopter and needing to leave, she'd had the opportunity to text Reese. Hopefully the call and the text would be enough to save Belle and herself.

The last words he'd said before she disconnected the call came to mind once again and she held onto them like a lifeline. *"I love you, Kelley. I will find you."*

She knew he would. She had to believe it.

But she also needed to do what she could to save herself and Belle. She needed to fight through the pain and fuzziness in her head. Just in case Reese didn't find her in time.

She waited as Taynor untied Belle. He forced her to stand and shoved her toward Kelley who caught the girl by her hand before giving her a quick hug.

"We're going to be okay," Kelley whispered to Belle as she tried to comfort the girl whose face was streaked with tears.

Rocha stood by the back of the truck and held one of the doors open as Taynor shoved Kelley and Belle toward the vehicle. Rocha's phone rang again and he dug it out of his pocket and answered it. He listened to the caller. His gaze cut to Taynor then shifted away again like he didn't want Taynor to know what he was talking about.

Taynor paused in what he'd been doing as he watched Rocha who was still looking away. A change came over Taynor's face and he moved toward Rocha, leaving Belle and Kelley by the truck's bumper.

As Rocha turned back to Taynor, Kelley saw the glint of a barrel of a gun. Taynor had clearly been expecting it as he kicked the weapon out of Rocha's hand.

Rocha snarled and went for the gun, but Taynor lunged at Rocha and took him down to the ground. The pair rolled in the dirt, fists flying.

"I'm going to kill you," Rocha shouted as he slammed his fist against the side of Taynor's head.

"You won't get the chance," Taynor said as he hit Rocha with an uppercut.

Taynor was taller and packed more weight than Rocha who was fairly short for a man, slender and wiry. What Taynor held in height and weight, Rocha made up for in speed and agility.

Kelley pressed Belle back against the truck. "Get under the truck and hide, Belle," she said urgently.

Belle hesitated then did what Kelley told her to do. Kelley eased toward the men, her eye on them and the gun that was just out of their reach even though both of them were fighting to get to it.

When she saw her chance, she dove for the weapon.

Taynor saw her just as her fingers nearly closed on the gun. He aimed a kick at her head and she couldn't help a scream of pain as his boot smashed into her skull. Black moved in and out of her vision. She struggled to hold onto consciousness as she braced herself on her hands and knees.

The time Taynor had taken to kick Kelley cost him. Rocha grabbed Taynor's head and Rocha rammed his knee into Taynor's face.

Taynor shrieked while blood spouted from his nose. Rocha reached for the gun but Kelley, fighting through the pain and dizziness, lunged for it and knocked it several feet away from the men.

"You'll pay for that, bitch," Rocha shouted.

But then Taynor was fighting like a wild man, slamming his fist into Rocha's ear.

Still struggling, her mind spinning, Kelley tried to reach the weapon as the men fought. She cut her gaze in the direction of the gun. It was gone.

She looked up and saw Belle holding it and she had it pointed at the men. Her expression was fierce and filled with loathing.

Unable to stand, Kelley crawled toward Belle as the men shouted and hit each other. "Give me the gun, honey," Kelley said to Belle.

But Belle looked stiff and frozen in place. She held the weapon in both hands, her arms outstretched, but shaking from the weight of a grown man's gun. She was just a young girl and the gun had to be too heavy for her.

Kelley had almost reached the girl when Rocha snatched the gun away from Belle. The girl screamed as Rocha backhanded her and sent her sprawling. Belle's head struck the square end of the pick that Kelley had tried to get to earlier. She watched in horror as the girl's eyes rolled back and she went still.

Fury burned red hot inside Kelley and she cut her gaze to Rocha. She was going to kill him if it was the last thing she did.

Rocha's face twisted with hatred as he swung the gun in Taynor's direction.

Kelley looked to see Taynor get to his feet and stumble. Two shots went off in quick succession. One hit Taynor in the gut and he doubled over. The second hit him in the forehead and he collapsed.

Rocha had just murdered his foster brother.

Eyes flashing with malevolence, his face ugly with his fury, Rocha turned the gun on Kelley.

Chapter 20

The helicopter was already rising into the air as Reese slid on his earphones. His heart was in his throat as he looked out into the darkness while the helicopter retraced the path they had taken.

He wanted to press the pilot to hurry, as if they might find the right barn faster. He peered out of the helicopter searching the ground with his gaze. He frowned as he saw a structure with glints of light slipping through gaps in the wood planks that made up the walls.

"I think that's it," Reese said.

"I see it." Munoz gave a nod. "I'll call it in."

Holloway circled the helicopter around the barn. The only sign that it might be what they were looking for was the light coming from the barn. Nothing else was visible that might indicate anyone could be there.

Again the Holloway guided the helicopter down so that it was hovering over a field behind the barn. This time the craft had to hover higher due to mesquite bushes in the field, so Reese, John, and Munoz had to slide down a rope to the ground to get them close enough.

Once they were on the ground, they headed for the barn. Thanks to living in the Arizona desert and being able to see for miles, the flashing lights of the sheriff's department and Border Patrol vehicles could be seen some distance away.

John and Reese covered the front of the barn while Munoz stayed in the back. John and Reese stood to either side of the huge double doors and peeked through spaces between the weathered boards.

Reese scanned the interior of the barn. He saw a man's body lying to one side of a refrigerated truck with pictures of ice cream on the side panels.

Adrenaline surged through Reese. They'd found it. Belle and Kelley had to be here.

From the size of the man's body lying crumpled on the ground, it could have been Taynor.

Reese saw a movement from around the back of the truck and then a bald, clean-shaven man Reese had never seen before walked from behind the truck to the front. He opened the driver's side door.

"We need to go in before he gets a chance to drive that truck out of here," Reese said to John.

John gave a nod. "Let's go."

Reese radioed Munoz and then on the count of three, he and John kicked in the barn's double doors.

The bald man made it behind the wheel and gunned the engine. Reese and John took positions in front of the truck and aimed their weapons at the driver.

"Get out with your hands up!" Reese shouted.

The driver put the truck into gear, gunned the engine, and drove toward Reese and John.

They fired off their weapons, but the bald man managed to duck down behind the wheel and keep the truck going forward even as Reese and John riddled the front windshield with bullets. They were forced to jump out of the way as the big truck barreled past them.

Reese seized his chance and swung up onto the back of the truck and gripped one of the door handles as his feet found purchase on the bumper. Cool air smacked his face as the truck picked up speed.

He holstered his weapon then hung onto a vertical bar with both hands. John and the barn fell behind as the truck bounced over the uneven dirt road, hitting potholes and making it difficult to hold on. The truck's tires thrummed over a cattle guard and then the vehicle was charging down another dirt road.

As he held on to the vehicle with one hand, he fought to disengage the heavy metal latch that would open the back of the refrigerated truck. Every time the truck hit rough ground, Reese had to pause to maintain his grip.

He ground his teeth as he tried again to unlatch the back, but his position was awkward and he was finding it difficult to get a good grip on the latch's handle with just the three fingers of his left hand.

The truck hit a particularly large pothole and jostled Reese so hard that he almost lost his balance. He had to grab the bar with both hands and somehow he managed to hang on.

He heard sirens growing louder and the flash of red and blue lights bouncing off the mesquite bushes lining the dirt road. He set his jaw and grasped the latch handle again. With all his strength, he pulled at it and felt something give so fast that he almost lost his balance again.

The heavy door swung open and Reese slipped his body into the opening. Ice-cold air hit him and goose bumps rose on his skin. The door swung back and hit him from behind, almost knocking the breath from him.

Pinned between the doors, he the steadied himself and looked inside. It was so dark that he couldn't see into the depths. He held on with one hand while fumbling for his slim flashlight from his belt with the three fingers of his left hand.

He gritted his teeth as the heavy door bounced against his back and he lost his grip on the flashlight. It dropped with a clatter onto the metal floor and rolled. He swore and tried to look inside. From what moonlight leaked in through the opening, he could see no one and he heard nothing.

Likely, Kelley and Belle had to be hidden in compartments somewhere inside or else they'd freeze to death and that wasn't what Rocha and Taynor had planned.

He considered climbing inside and grabbing the flashlight to look for them, but it wouldn't do a damn bit of good for him to freeze to death if he was unable to get the door open from the inside to get out again. Likely they were in insulated compartments somewhere in the truck.

The heavy door at his back made it almost impossible to slip out. With effort, he extricated himself and barely missed having his hand pinned by the door.

Outside the refrigerated truck was positively warm compared to the inside. He inched over so that he could see in front of them.

Sheriff's department and Border Patrol vehicles blocked the road ahead. The man driving the truck didn't slow down. If anything, he drove faster.

Reese braced himself for impact.

The truck crashed into the law enforcement vehicles. Sounds of weapons being fired, metal screeching, glass shattering, and the shouts of officers filled the night.

Reese barely heard the noise as the truck started to tilt to one side. It was going down. He jumped off the back and landed on the ground on his shoulder. He felt it dislocate as he rolled and he ground his teeth from the shrieking pain now radiating through him.

He scrambled to his feet and gritting his teeth, he pulled his arm and jerked it back into place. The pain was nothing compared to his fear for Kelley as the huge truck flipped onto its side.

The truck skidded to a stop, resting on its side. Despite the pain in his shoulder, Reese bolted toward the truck, drawing his weapon as he ran. He heard the shouts of other police officers approaching, but they were coming from behind him.

When he neared the truck, the man who'd been driving rose out of the driver's side window. He raised a weapon and started shooting.

Reese felt a bullet graze his shoulder. He dropped to one knee, steadied himself, and fired off three shots. The man slumped forward, hanging half in and half out of the truck, still gripping his gun.

Cautiously, Reese moved forward, training his weapon on the man who remained still. Just as Reese approached, the bald man rose. He aimed his weapon at Reese who shot the man again.

This time when the man collapsed, his gun slid from his fingers and landed on the ground with a thump.

In moments, the sheriff and his deputies arrived along with the Border Patrol agents, John, and Munoz, and two German shepherds. The deputies took over the scene at the head of the truck. Someone checked the man's pulse and verified that he was dead.

Reese, John, and the Border Patrol agents took the back. The agents shone flashlights inside the seemingly empty truck. Reese saw his own flashlight shining from what was now the floor of the truck.

The agents turned the shepherds loose. They both ran inside and started barking at two sections of what was the floor that was now on its side. Reese and the agents went into the freezing interior and searched for compartments where Kelley and Belle must be hidden.

The compartments were so well hidden that it took some time to find any seams in the metal. One of the agents grabbed a crowbar from his vehicle and Reese took it to pry open the panel.

Pain ricocheted through Reese's body as he attempted to pry the panel open, especially the shoulder he'd dislocated. He gritted his teeth and only worked harder at it. A scrape of metal and then the panel moved a little. Another agent brought in another crowbar, and together they pried off the panel.

Kelley slid out of the exposed compartment. Reese caught her to him, holding her tightly, never wanting to let go.

"Reese." Relief was in her voice as she clung to him. "Thank God. Thank you for finding us."

"I would never have given up until I did," he said fiercely. "I don't care how long and hard, I would have found you."

She drew away as he set her on her feet. "I know you would have. I never doubted it." Panic crossed her features. "Belle. Where is she?" Kelley looked at the agents who were working on prying open another panel. "Belle. I need to see her." Kelley sounded horrified. "She hit her head on a pickaxe. Is she alive?"

"We don't know yet," Reese said. She started toward the agents, but Reese held her back. "Give them a moment to get the compartment open."

"If she's still alive, I need to be the first person Belle sees." Kelley tried to pull away from Reese, but he kept a grip on her, holding her to him by her shoulders.

Metal screeched again as the panel began to rise. Reese and Kelley moved toward the compartment. "We've had a hell of a time getting the compartments open," Reese said. "They must have some kind of release that we can't see."

The moment the panel was removed, Kelley was there to see the girl open her eyes, a dazed expression on her features.

Reese helped Kelley reach for Belle. Kelley brought Belle into her arms and held her tightly.

"It's all over." Kelley rocked the girl who began sobbing. "They'll never hurt you again."

Belle raised her tear-stained face and looked up at Kelley. "Thank you for saving me."

"Reese came for us. But if it wasn't for your phone, it would have been a lot harder." Kelley brushed tears away from Belle's face. "You helped save us."

The girl gripped Kelley's neck again then went limp.

"Belle." Tears rolled down Kelley's face. "Belle, wake up."

Reese touched his fingers to Belle's neck. "Her heartbeat is steady. We'll get her to the hospital now." He took the girl from Kelley's arms and they hurried toward one of the waiting sheriff's department cruisers.

"I'm going with her," Kelley said with a defiant expression.

"We'll both go with her." Reese slid in with Belle in his arms.

Kelley slid onto the seat beside Reese and she reached for Belle's hand.

The deputy started driving away from the scene, lights flashing in the night.

"Taynor is dead, too." Kelley's voice was thick. "I would have liked to kill them both myself."

"Damn, but I love you, Kelley." Reese stroked her tangled hair from her face. Her hair was matted with blood. "I was so afraid I'd lose you."

She met his gaze. "I love you, Reese." She rested her head on his chest as she gripped Belle's hand. "I love you," she whispered again before she passed out.

CHAPTER 21

Reese and Kelley sat by Belle's hospital bed, Kelley holding the girl's hand. Belle's head was bandaged and her face looked pale, her dark eyelashes stark against the whiteness of her skin.

A doctor had attended to Kelley's and Reese's injuries, but they'd both refused hospital beds. After they were treated, Kelley insisted on staying by Belle's hospital bed, waiting for the girl to wake up.

Reese hadn't let Kelley out of his sight. The sheriff's deputies had taken his and Kelley's statements in Belle's hospital room.

Kelley stroked her thumb over Belle's hand. She looked at Reese. "Belle's been out of it for so long."

Reese put his arm around Kelley's shoulders and kissed the top of her head. "She's going to be okay. The doctor said she's fine."

With a nod, Kelley turned back to Belle. Her heart stumbled as the girl stirred. Reese moved his arm from around Kelley as Belle's eyelids fluttered open. The girl frowned as she looked around the room before her confused gaze rested on Kelley. The moment Belle met Kelley's eyes the confused look vanished.

"Are you okay?" Belle asked.

Surprised that it was the first thing Belle said, Kelley smiled. "I'm fine, honey. You're going to be okay, too."

Belle put her hand to her bandaged forehead. "My head aches."

"It probably will for some time." Kelley squeezed the girl's hand. "You hit your head pretty hard."

"Okay." Belle seemed to realize for the first time that Reese was there and she looked at him.

"Hi, Belle," he said.

"You rescued us," she said.

He smiled. "With your help."

Belle's gaze flitted back to meet Kelley's. "I'm tired."

Kelley brushed the back of her hand over Belle's forehead. "You get some sleep."

"Stay with me," Belle said.

"I'll be right here." Kelley squeezed Belle's hand again. "I'm not going anywhere."

"Okay." Belle's eyelids fluttered closed and she drifted off to sleep.

"She doesn't have a mother anymore, and that sorry excuse for a man could never be called a father." Kelley looked at Reese. "I'm glad he's dead after all he put her through."

Reese put his arm around Kelley's shoulders again. "His death was no more than he deserved."

Kelley nodded slowly. "I want to adopt Belle."

Reese didn't look surprised. "I think that's a great idea."

She smiled at him before leaning toward him and resting her head on his chest as he held her to him.

* * * * *

Two weeks after they brought Belle back to Prescott, Kelley knelt on the grass beside Belle, next to Laura's grave. The white headstone shone in the bright sunshine as Belle placed a bouquet of flowers at the base.

She looked at Kelley. "I miss my mom."

"I know you do." Kelley stroked Belle's hair from her face. "I understand how you feel, more than you know."

Belle's forehead wrinkled. "Did your mom die, too?"

Kelley picked at a blade of grass as she thought about what she should say. The truth seemed to be the best course. "My father killed my mother when I was a teenager." The memory of her mother was sharp and clear.

"Like my dad killed my mom." Belle's face fell. "But he wasn't like a real dad. And then he—and then—" A tear rolled down her cheek.

Kelley put her arm around Belle's shoulders. "He'll never hurt you again."

"I know." Another tear. "What happened to your dad?"

Kelley looked away before returning her gaze to Belle's. "He's in prison. He's dying from lung cancer."

Belle studied Kelley's face. "Are you glad?"

For a moment Kelley thought about it. "I wanted him to rot in prison. Now that he's dying from cancer… To be honest, I'm not sure how I feel."

"I'm glad my dad is dead." Belle said the words with a fierce intensity. "He deserved it."

Kelley said nothing, just studied Belle.

"Do you have any other family?" Belle asked. "Other than your dad?"

"Yes." Kelley thought about her grandmother's visit. "My grandmother... My dad's mother."

"I don't have any family." Belle looked lost. "I don't like my foster mother and father." She bit her lower lip. "I want to live with you."

"I was going to talk to you about that." Kelley smiled. "I want to adopt you. Would that be okay with you?"

A smile lit up Belle's face. "Yes!" She glanced at her mother's headstone before meeting Kelley's gaze. "I think Mom would like that."

Kelley smiled, too. "I've been working on it, but I wanted to make sure you'd like that."

"Yes," Belle said again as she nodded. "When can I move in with you?"

"Once we get through all of the red tape," Kelley said, "I'll be able to take you home with me."

Belle beamed.

"So be sure and be good for your foster parents," Kelley continued. "I'll keep visiting you until the paperwork goes through and you can come home with me."

Kelley glanced at the rows of headstones in the cemetery, thinking about her mother's grave in Phoenix. When she looked back at Belle, she said, "Are you ready to go?"

Belle's gaze rested on her mother's grave. She sobered a bit before she nodded. "Yes."

Taking Belle by the hand, Kelley stood and brought the girl to her feet along with her. Sunshine warmed their shoulders as they walked away from the cemetery together.

* * * * *

As she neared the state penitentiary in Florence, Kelley pressed the number on her cell phone for Dolores Petrova.

A sharp voice answered her call. "Yes?"

"Hi, Grandmother," Kelley said quietly.

A pause before the elder woman said, "Have you come to your senses?"

Kelley tried not to bristle. Next to her father, her grandmother was her only living relative. "I'm on my way to the prison to see him," Kelley said, holding back the retort she wanted to make.

"Good." Dolores's voice softened. "He deserves another chance."

Kelley let out her breath, surprised at her grandmother's soft tone. It didn't matter that Kelley didn't agree. What mattered was that she needed closure.

"Would you like to go out to lunch sometime?" Kelley asked Dolores.

Another pause before her grandmother said, "I would like that."

"Are you free next Sunday for lunch?" Kelley asked. "I can make it down to Phoenix."

"Yes." Dolores hesitated. "Yes, that would be nice."

"I'll call you Saturday," Kelley said before she told her grandmother goodbye and disconnected the call.

When Kelley reached the prison she parked and went into the building where she signed in and presented her service weapon. She was accompanied to the visitor's area where she was seated in front of a glass wall with dividers between her and the other visitors. An empty chair was on the other side of the wall.

She wouldn't have recognized the wasted man who shuffled in, handcuffed and hobbled, if she hadn't known it was her father. Isaac Petrova was thin and gaunt, looking far older than his fifty plus years. At that moment she wasn't sure she should even be there. Why was she here?

Closure. She needed to see him one last time.

After he seated himself, they each picked up their receivers. For a long moment they looked at each other, his once vibrant blue eyes that had been so like hers now dulled.

"What are you doing here?" he finally said.

"I wanted to see the man who killed my mother one last time." Kelley studied him. "I never had the chance to tell you what I felt when you destroyed our lives. And I want to know why you killed her."

Isaac looked away before he turned his gaze on her again. "I hear you're a detective now."

Thrown off guard, she gripped the receiver tighter. "How do you know that?"

"Your grandmother." His eyes suddenly seemed clearer. "She's proud of you, you know."

No, she hadn't known that, hadn't known it at all. Kelley cleared her throat. "I went into law enforcement because of you and what you did to Mom and me. Especially because of what you did to Mom. I help those who are hurt by people like you and try to save them before it's too late." Like her own mother…and Laura. She'd failed them both. She wondered if someday she could forgive herself.

Isaac looked down at his free hand. His knuckles were white on the hand that held his receiver. He met her gaze. "I'm sorry how

I treated you and your mother." His voice was thick. "I'm sorry I killed her."

Kelley felt nothing as he spoke. She'd hated this man with a passion so deep that it had stayed with her every day of her life. "Why did you kill her?"

His free hand flexed. "I didn't mean to."

"Yes, you did." Her voice was harsh to her own ears, the sound seeming to echo in the receiver. "When I left, you blamed her and you killed her."

"I'm so sorry." His throat worked. "Can you forgive me?"

She slowly shook her head. "Only God can forgive you for what you've done. It's not up to me."

"I'm dying," he said. "I have lung cancer."

"I know." Kelley realized she now felt nothing for this pitiful man. "Grandmother told me."

"I'm a born again Christian now." He seemed to recover. "I accepted Jesus. He died on the cross to save people like me. To save us all."

Kelley held his gaze. "If you can die believing that, then you have more than you deserve."

"I do believe it." He gave a slow nod. "If He can forgive me, why can't you?"

"Goodbye, Isaac." She hung up the receiver and gave him one last look before she rose from her seat and turned away.

She felt his gaze on her back as one of the jailors led her back to the front entrance to the prison. She continued to see his wasted face as she took back her service weapon and signed out.

The fact that she no longer felt a burning hatred for Isaac Petrova made her wonder. Had she forgiven him?

It didn't matter. All that mattered was now she could move on. Now she could put what had happened to her mother over fifteen years ago behind her and walk away.

The future suddenly seemed brighter now that she could let her past rest, now that the weight had been lifted from her shoulders.

Yes, now she could move on.

CHAPTER 22

Kelley followed Johan's instructions for another exercise to strengthen her shoulder with more resistance and repetitions than ever before.

"What a way to start out the morning." She groaned at the burning ache. "Don't get me wrong, but I'll be glad when I don't have to see you anymore."

He grinned. "You've come a long way."

"The doc cleared me to return to work on Monday." She blew out her breath. "The past few weeks have been enough of a break as far as I'm concerned."

Johan rested his hand on her upper back as she continued with another rep. "Another couple of weeks and you will be finished here."

She smirked. "I'll be beyond happy to be done with your torturous training."

He laughed. "I've got a little more in store for you just to make sure you remember me."

"How could I forget?" she said before he showed her the new exercises. She gritted her teeth as she finished her reps.

Johan squeezed her uninjured shoulder. "Good job, Kelley."

As they finished up, she felt heat on her back and a prickle at her nape. It wasn't unpleasant, but it caused her to turn around. Reese was watching. When their gazes met, he smiled.

She raised her hand in a little wave as she returned his smile. "Almost done," she said.

"Did I ever tell you what a good-looking man you have, Detective Petrova?" Johan asked with a cocky grin. "If he wasn't yours I would consider him fair game."

Kelley snorted back a laugh. "I'm quite sure Reese doesn't swing that way." She couldn't help a grin. "But the point is moot since he's all mine."

Johan grinned back as Reese moved toward them.

"Hi, Detective McBride." Johan held out his hand.

Reese took it and gave a nod. "How's she doing?" he asked as they released hands.

"Not much longer until she's all yours again." Johan said with a mischievous look.

Reese raised a brow but amusement was in his eyes. "She's already all mine."

"*She* is sitting right here," Kelley said with mock exasperation.

"If she's ready to go, I'll take her off your hands now," Reese said to Johan, ignoring Kelley's response.

Johan gave a nod then smiled at Kelley. "I'll see you at your next appointment."

"Speaking of appointments," Reese said as he and Kelley left the physical therapy gym, "it's almost time for our appointment with Captain Johnson."

She groaned. "I'm really not looking forward to this."

"I know what you mean," Reese said, "but it's time we come clean, before you return to work on Monday."

"I guess we've put it off as long as possible." She sighed. "I hope he doesn't blow a gasket over this and that we end up with our jobs intact."

Once they were in Reese's truck and on their way, it didn't take them long to get to the police station. It was a beautiful morning filled with sunshine, the summer heat already starting to rise.

Kelley felt half dread and half elation at telling their captain about their relationship. She couldn't help the feeling of elation that flowed through her at the thought of her love for Reese and his love for her.

When Reese knocked on the doorframe of Captain Reginald Johnson's office, the captain waved them in. Reese closed the door to the office behind him before he and Kelley settled into the two chairs in front of the captain's desk.

Johnson looked from Reese to Kelley. "What can I do for you two?"

Kelley opened her mouth to tell the captain then looked at Reese. He gave a single nod. She returned her gaze to meet Johnson's. "Reese and I have—have developed a relationship."

The captain studied them. "A relationship."

She nodded. "Beyond being co-workers and partners."

"I see." Johnson leaned back in his chair and folded his hands on his belly. His keen gray eyes looked from Kelley to Reese and back. "How long has this been going on?"

Kelley's stomach flipped and she glanced at Reese. His gaze remained steady as he said, "Not until Kelley went on leave."

"You mean the leave where she continued to work a case when she was supposed to be off of it?" Johnson said.

"Yes." Kelley swallowed. "Around that time."

Johnson looked serious as he folded his hands on his desk. A long moment of silence passed that had Kelley's heart thumping.

Finally, the captain said, "I'll be assigning you new partners, of course."

Kelley let out her breath and she felt Reese relax beside her. "Yes, Captain," she said and Reese nodded.

"You're two of the best detectives this force has ever seen." Captain Johnson smiled. "For what it's worth, you have my blessing."

"That's worth a lot, Captain," Kelley said.

Johnson picked up a pen and tapped it on his desk. "If you'd carried this on while you were on the job, this conversation might not have gone so well."

"Yes, sir," Kelley said. "That would never have happened."

Johnson pushed away from his desk and stood. Reese and Kelley got to their feet, too. Johnson held out his hand to Kelley who took it. He squeezed her hand before releasing it and shaking Reese's, too.

"You come back to work Monday," Johnson said to Kelley and she nodded. "I'll give you your new assignments then."

"Yes, sir," Kelley and Reese replied.

Johnson waved them out of his office and Kelley breathed a huge sigh of relief as she and Reese headed through the station.

"Thank God that went well," she said when they reached the front doors.

"What do you say to a stay in a bed and breakfast in Williams this weekend?" Reese asked as they strode out into the sunshine. "We'll go to the Grand Canyon."

"I'd say that sounds like a great idea." She smiled at him. "I haven't been to the Grand Canyon in forever. When do we leave?"

"How about noon?" he asked.

She laughed. "That's in an hour."

"Yep." They reached his truck. "You'd better get packed."

She raised her brows. "What were you going to do if I said no?"

"I'd planned to take you whether or not you said yes." He opened up the door to his truck and she climbed in. "But I knew you wouldn't say no."

She rolled her eyes. "You McBrides are so arrogant."

He flashed a grin. "We just know what we want."

She couldn't help a smile as he closed the truck door and she settled into her seat. Reese might be an arrogant McBride, but he was *her* arrogant McBride.

* * * * *

Williams was billed as the "Gateway to the Grand Canyon," and Kelley liked the town and loved the area. At an elevation of 7,000 feet, the bed & breakfast Reese had chosen was nestled in the juniper and pine at the foot of Bill Williams Mountain.

It was early afternoon when they arrived at the B & B. When they climbed out of the truck, Kelley breathed in the scents of fresh air, pine, and loam. She loved the sweet, clean smells as they unloaded their bags from the truck and carried them inside.

The owner greeted them as they stepped inside the B & B. The entryway was quaint with rich wood flooring and cornflower blue walls with wallpaper that had tiny sprigs of pink roses. Once they'd checked in with the matronly woman and had taken their things to their room, Kelley and Reese headed for the South Rim of the Grand Canyon.

By the time they reached their destination and parked, the sun was sliding down the western sky. A light wind tugged at her blouse and whipped her hair around her face and it was starting to cool.

Reese took Kelley's hand and they walked up a slope to the visitor's area. Once they stood behind the barrier at the edge of the rim, he took her hand. His grip felt warm and firm, as if he'd never let her go.

Kelley's breath caught as she looked out at the magnificent view. It was beyond awe-inspiring, nearly overwhelming, the magnitude of the canyon almost beyond human comprehension. She squeezed his hand as if somehow that would tell him how she was feeling at that moment.

The geological colors of rich red, brown, faded cream, and an almost purplish shade, were utterly beautiful. The width and breadth of the canyon were staggering to view and it was difficult to believe that such an incredible wonder could exist today. From a previous trip to the canyon, she'd learned it was over two hundred and seventy-five river miles long, eighteen miles wide, and up to a mile deep.

While she took in the awe-inspiring view, Reese put his arm around her shoulders. She loved the feel of his embrace and she tipped her head against his chest as they drank in their surroundings.

"I brought you here for a reason." He squeezed her to him.

She drew back and looked up at him, into his brilliant blue gaze, and she smiled. "More than the amazing view?"

He nodded, slowly. "You are the one who's amazing."

The breeze tossed her hair about her face and she brushed strands from her eyes. "Funny, but I think the same about you. You are utterly amazing."

"Kelley…" He trailed off for a moment and she tilted her head to the side. "I don't know why I didn't realize it sooner, why it took two years after you became my partner… Or maybe I did realize it, but wasn't ready to recognize it for what it was." He paused. "You were made for me and I was made for you."

She felt a warmth in her belly that spread throughout her from the tips of her toes to the roots of her hair. "Yes," she said quietly. "That's it, exactly."

He slipped his hand into his front pocket and he lowered himself to one knee she saw him pull out a small black velvet box. Her eyes widened. Her hands started to shake and she brought her palm to her mouth. He opened the box and nestled in black velvet was a simple diamond solitaire.

"Marry me, Kelley." His gaze was sincere and filled with a kind of hope she'd never seen there before. "I want to be with you for the rest of our lives."

She lowered her hand. For a moment she felt beyond words and could not speak. He looked so loving, so hopeful, as if everything he wanted in the world rested in her answer.

Her voice trembled as she nodded. "Yes." She smiled as a grin split his features. "I would marry you a thousand times over."

He slipped the ring onto her finger then rose and took her into his arms. "I love you, honey. I love you so damned much."

"And I love you." She held onto him tightly as they stood next to the rim of the canyon, her love for him expanding beyond the width and breadth of the place. She couldn't imagine loving anyone as much as she loved him.

She wrapped her arms around his neck as he kissed her hard. Joy spread throughout her entire being as she kissed him back with everything she had.

When they parted and looked into each other's eyes, she said, "I've never been this happy in my life. Ever."

He pressed his lips to her forehead. "You are everything to me and I know I've never been happier."

"How do you feel about a ready-made family?" Kelley smiled as she took his hands in hers. "Belle's adoption will go through soon."

"I think we should get married right away." He squeezed her hands. "Then Belle will have a mother and a father to love her."

"I know she'll love that." Kelley felt an excitement building inside her. "What do you say about Las Vegas?"

He tugged on a lock of her hair. "I say that Las Vegas sounds perfect."

"Good." She smiled. "That's settled."

They turned and faced the Grand Canyon as he settled his arm around her shoulders, holding her to him as she rested her head against his chest. The magnitude of the moment went even further than the magnitude of the sight that lay before them. Happiness filled her and expanded beyond what could not be comprehended, beyond what filled one's soul with awe.

To two lives entwined and as ever lasting as what had existed for millennia and what would continue to exist forevermore.

CHAPTER 23

Kelley felt a swooping sensation as Reese carried her over the threshold of their Las Vegas suite. She laughed as he took off each of her high-heeled shoes and tossed them over his shoulder. As he lowered her beside the large bed, her silky sapphire blue dress slid to her upper thighs as he put her down before it fell to just above her knees again.

When he'd proposed to her yesterday, she'd thought she'd never be happier. But she was now, impossibly so. They had driven straight from Williams this morning. While she went shopping at a boutique for attire appropriate for a Las Vegas wedding, he'd gone to a western clothing store.

They'd tied the knot a mere hour ago but it felt like they'd been husband and wife for as long as she could remember.

"You are so beautiful, Detective McBride," Reese said with a grin as he settled his hands on her hips.

She returned his grin and reached up to take off his cream-colored Stetson, which she tossed on a nearby chair. "You aren't so bad yourself, Detective McBride," she said as she ruffled his hair.

And he wasn't bad at all. With his now mussed light brown hair, his vivid blue eyes and square features, not to mention the sensual curve of his lips…he was one of the sexiest men she'd ever had the pleasure of knowing.

He kissed her soundly, shutting down all thoughts in her mind of anything but being in his arms at that moment.

His kiss turned into something even more passionate and she matched his intensity. The desire to have him inside her was strong and it was all she could do to keep from ripping his western shirt open and unbuckling his belt.

She gave a little sigh as he moved his lips down her throat. Her sigh turned into a moan while he rubbed his thumbs over her nipples in circles that nearly took her breath away.

Even as she squirmed in his arms, he seemed determined to take it slow. She wanted him with an urgency that bordered on the frantic but she let him set the pace. She fell into it with a wanton abandon as he sent her mind spinning with desire.

He kissed lower, to where the neckline of her dress ended just above her breasts. She gave a little shudder of need as he dipped his tongue into her cleavage, teasing the sensitive skin between her breasts. She wanted more of him, needed more of him.

She shivered as he reached behind her and tugged down her dress's zipper that traveled all the way down to the base of her spine. He pushed the dress over her shoulders and she let it slide down her arms before it dropped to the floor in a shimmering blue puddle. She stepped out of it and he carefully set the dress on the chair next to his Stetson.

He returned his gaze to her, looking like a man dying of thirst as he let his gaze drift over her petite form. She wore a black bra, as well as black panties and a garter with sheer stockings that she had purchased at the boutique to go under the dress she had been wearing.

When he met her eyes again, he said, "You know that you're my everything, Kelley."

She touched the side of his face, feeling the stubble along his jaws with her fingertips. "You are an amazing man. I feel blessed to have you at my side."

He kissed her again, gripping her by her waist and drawing her up against him. She felt his erection pressing into her bare belly and the ache that had begun to grow between her thighs became sharper. He trailed his fingertips along the curve of her satiny bra and she gave a little gasp as he tugged her bra down, exposing her breasts.

With a rumble deep in his throat, he lowered his head and suckled first one nipple then the other. She slid her fingers into his soft hair and tipped her head back as the erotic sensations spread from her breasts to tingle in every part of her body.

He unfastened her bra and slid it down her arms then tossed the bra aside. He trailed his fingers from the curves of her breasts, down her sides to the top of her garters. "Let's leave these on."

She moaned as he slid his finger between her thighs over the damp satiny material covering her folds.

"I almost can't believe you're mine." He moved his hands up and pushed his fingers into her hair and cupped the back of her head. "My beautiful, intelligent, sexy, kick-ass wife."

She would have grinned if he weren't doing such sensual things to her body. His every kiss, his every touch, was pure magic.

The fact that he still had clothes on made no sense to her at that moment. She reached for his cream-colored western shirt and ripped apart the pearl snaps, exposing the expanse of his muscular chest. She pushed the shirt over his shoulders and he shrugged out of it so that it fell to the floor.

Her heart beat faster as he toed off his boots and kicked them aside. In moments he had peeled his socks off and she reached for his silver belt buckle. She didn't fumble as she undid the belt and then she was unzipping his black western dress slacks. She pushed down his slacks and his boxer briefs and he stepped out of them.

A sigh of pleasure escaped her when she reached for his cock. The soft skin felt silky over the hard length that she wanted to more than touch, she wanted to taste it too. But he seemed more intent on feeling her body against his, the heat of their need making it almost too much to bear.

He scooped her up in his arms, catching her by surprise, and carried her to the huge bed at the center of the room. He laid her on the bed and looked down at her. She felt warmth upon her skin, everywhere his gaze touched her.

"Come to me." She held out her arms to him.

He lowered himself so that his arms were braced to either side of her.

His jaw tightened as he held himself still. "What do you say we give Belle a little brother or sister?"

Kelley smiled. "I say that sounds perfect."

His hips spread her thighs further apart. He pulled aside the panties of her garter, exposing her folds.

She reached between them and grasped his cock, guiding him into her core. She gasped with pleasure as he filled her, his length driving so deep he reached her G-spot. He began rocking in and out of her, his cock making her crazy with the need to climax. He took her slowly, making love to her with his body and his eyes.

His strokes became firmer and harder and she moaned as she grew closer and closer to climax. She felt as if her mind was spinning, need growing inside her like a living thing that would soon take over her body and mind.

And then her body seemed to explode with heat and fire. She cried out, not caring about anything but the man between her thighs and her love and passion for him. Lights and colors flashed in her vision.

As she came down from her high, her core continued to spasm around his cock as he moved in and out of her. She looked into the face she loved and saw the fierceness in his expression.

She reached between them and brushed his balls with her fingertips and he seemed to explode, too, as he came hard. He closed his eyes as he thrust and his jaw was tense, his expression as fiery as the flames of her orgasm which continued to heat her body as he moved in and out.

And then he pressed his body tightly to hers and it was as if they were one, joined together in more ways than only marriage.

With a groan he took her into his arms, rolling with her and keeping her close to him. As he tucked her next to him, she felt something that she hadn't felt since her mother passed away. It was a feeling of coming home, of having a refuge to go to whenever she needed one.

"I love you so very much, Reese." She snuggled more fully against him. "I can't imagine having anyone in my life who I could possibly love more than I love you."

He kissed her forehead. "You are an amazing woman, Kelley. I know I've said it before but I'll say it again. I love you more than I have words to say."

And with that she smiled and knew that she had her happy ending.

ALSO BY CHEYENNE MCCRAY

"Dark Enforcers" Series

Night's Captive

Lexi Steele Novels

The First Sin

The Second Betrayal

The Temptation

~Romantic Erotica~

"Seraphine Chronicles" Series

Forbidden

Bewitched

Spellbound

(Spellbound includes bonus novella, *Untamed)*

Possessed

From St. Martin's Press:

"Night Tracker" Series

Demons Not Included

No Werewolves Allowed

Vampires Not Invited

Zombies Sold Separately

Vampires Dead Ahead

"Magic" Series

Forbidden Magic

Seduced by Magic

Wicked Magic

Shadow Magic

Dark Magic

Single Title

Moving Target

Chosen Prey

Anthologies

No Rest for the Witches

Real Men Last All Night

Legally Hot

Chicks Kick Butt

Hotter than Hell

Mammoth Book of Paranormal Romances

Mammoth Book of Special Ops Romances

EXCERPT... HOT FOR YOU

Cheyenne McCray

She had just finished her third mojito when Cody asked her to dance. He took her by the hand and led her to the dance floor. She felt a little tipsy and warm inside but was still steady on her feet.

It was a slow song, and Cody brought her in close to him as she put her hands on his shoulders. A fluttering sensation batted around in her belly and her heart beat a little faster as she felt his body heat even though there was a good inch between them.

His beautiful warm brown eyes studied her. "Enjoying yourself?"

She hoped he couldn't see the sudden nervousness that gripped her. "Yes. I like your cousins and their wives."

The corner of his mouth tipped up. "There's plenty more where they came from."

She smiled in return and he brought her in closer so that their bodies were touching and she caught her breath. She linked her hands around his neck as he moved his own hands to her hips.

Heat rose inside her and her throat grew dry as their gazes held. He looked at her lips as if he wanted to kiss her. She wanted him to more than she'd ever wanted a kiss before. Her tongue darted out to touch her lips and he brought her body flush with his.

The hard ridge of his erection pressed against her belly. An ache grew between her thighs and her nipples grew taut. She had the sudden desire to take him by the hand, lead him out of the club, and tell him to drive home as fast as possible.

She wanted him. And she wanted him now.

Someone ran into her from behind and she fell forward against Cody. She looked over her shoulder but the couples around them seemed to be paying attention only to their partners. It was the second time that night that someone had run into her, but this time there wasn't a guy trying to apologize to her.

"Don't get me wrong," Cody said as she looked back at him. He was grinning as he held her tight. "But you don't have to throw yourself at me."

Heat warmed her cheeks. "Someone bumped into me."

He just smiled, a slow sensual smile that curled her toes.

The slow song was winding down and she didn't want it to stop. Without realizing that she was doing it, she moved up onto her tiptoes and he lowered his head.

When his lips met hers, it was like fireworks went off in her belly and in her mind. Vaguely she was aware that a faster tune had started playing, but still Cody kissed her. It was a long, slow kiss that sent thrills from where their lips met straight to her toes.

She was breathing hard when they parted and she looked into his eyes that glittered in the low lighting.

His throat worked as he held her gaze. "Ready to go home?" His voice was husky.

She only hesitated a moment before she gave a single nod. He put his palm on her lower back and guided her through the crowd of dancers.

Excerpt... Crazy For You

Cheyenne McCray

The afternoon was growing long as she reached a stock tank, not too far from a small thicket of oak and mesquite trees. She dismounted and let Poca drink from the tank.

Ella felt a prickling along her spine and looked around to see a horse and rider approaching. Clint. A strange combination of irritation and pleasure traveled up and down her spine. Irritation that he had followed her, and pleasure that he was there. Then irritation at her pleasure.

Frowning, she turned her attention to Poca, ignoring Clint. Out of the corner of her eye she watched him dismount Charger when they reached the tank and then lead his horse to the water. She noticed a blanket rolled up on the back of Charger's saddle.

She glanced at him. "What are you doing out here?"

"Checking up on you." He said the words casually.

She scowled at him. "What right do you have—?"

In the next moment he gripped her upper arms so tightly that she caught her breath in surprise. The look in his brown eyes caused her heart to pound and she dropped Poca's reins to brace her palms on Clint's chest, ready to push him away.

He had never looked as handsome as he did that moment, his expression so intense that she felt as if she might be consumed by the need she felt emanating from him. A raw, powerful need that she shared with every part of her being.

She swallowed as flutters traveled through her belly. "Let me go, Clint."

His expression turned serious, but he didn't let her go. "I have one question for you. Whether or not I let you go depends on the answer to that question."

She raised an eyebrow. "And that would be?"

"What's your relationship with Johnny Parker?" he said slowly.

Confused by his question, she blinked. "We're good friends. Why?"

"That's all I needed to hear." He dragged her up against him and his mouth came down hard on hers.

Completely caught off guard, she let out a startled gasp, but he swallowed it with his kiss. It was powerful and demanding as he slipped his tongue into her mouth and he gripped her ass in his big hands. His cock was hard as he held her tightly to him.

The thought of struggling came to a quick death as she fell into the kiss. She gave a soft moan as he ground his erection against her belly and she felt an answering tingle between her thighs. Not just a tingle but a full on explosion of need and desire. She thought about the night he had touched her and brought her to orgasm and she gave a soft moan.

She grew lightheaded, as if she needed more oxygen. When he drew away she stared up into his eyes. "I need to finish checking the fence line." The words came out in a husky whisper, as if she wasn't sure about herself, not at all like she'd intended.

"You need to stay right here." He moved his lips to her ear. "With me."

A shiver traveled down her spine. "No." She swallowed. "I need to—"

He took her mouth hard again and she felt every bit of resolve slipping. How many times had she dreamed of his kisses? And now that she was a grown woman, here she was, in his arms.

Her whole body felt like soft clay, as if he could mold her, shape her, make her a work of art with his touches and kisses. He groaned deep and low in his throat and she shivered again as he moved his palms from her ass to her waist and back again. His hands felt sure and strong, and she felt a sense of possessiveness running through him, as if she belonged to no other.

No, he was just trying to change her mind and she couldn't allow him to get away with that.

She shoved at him hard, breaking the kiss, severing the fire that had made her feel connected to him in ways she couldn't have imagined. "That's enough."

"I'm just getting started." He caught her up in his embrace so that his arm was beneath her ass and she was halfway over his shoulder.

She struggled in his arms. "Put me down, Clint." He was so strong that she could barely move.

He held on to her with one arm and with his other he unbuckled two straps holding the rolled up blanket on the back of Charger's saddle.

It occurred to her then exactly what he planned to do with that blanket. She tried to get away but he carried her to the thicket of oak and mesquite trees. He unfurled the blanket on the ground with his free arm, at the base of a group of rocks that were beneath the trees.

He turned and twisted her in the air and she let out a surprised cry as he sat on one of the big rocks. In the next moment she found herself laying facedown, over his knees, her arms pinned behind her back, her hair hanging over her face.

"You deserve a spanking for being so damned difficult," he growled.

A spanking? Hell no. "Let me go, Clint. Or I swear you'll regret it."

"Be still." He held her wrists in one hand then swatted her hard with his other.

The sting caused her to cry out and her eyes watered. "Don't!" Again he swatted her and again she cried out. "Stop it!"

To her shock, she felt a tingling between her thighs as he spanked her. She didn't know how it could be, but with every swat she pictured him thrusting inside her. Her breasts ached and her nipples were hard nubs. She wriggled and felt his rigid cock against her body.

He paused and rubbed her ass with his palm. "Will that make you be quiet and listen?"

"You're a big bully." She realized her breathing had quickened and a thrill had coiled deep in her belly. "I'll never be quiet with that kind of treatment."

"Is that so?" He swatted her again, harder this time, and she felt a greater tingling between her thighs. "I think you like it."

"Never." The more she fought him, the more turned on she was getting.

He moved his fingers between her thighs and she caught her breath. He had to feel her heat and maybe even how damp she was through her jeans.

Her head spun, her hair flying around her face, as he swept her up and held her to him. Automatically she wrapped her arms around his neck and her thighs around his waist and held on.

He laid her on her back on the blanket. She started to scramble away but he grabbed her leg and pulled her to him. She tried to kick free but he was on her, pinning her legs between his thighs and holding her wrists above her head as his big body pressed her to the makeshift bed.

She was pinned so securely that there was no struggling now. Before she could utter another word, he kissed her hard. At first she refused him, but she melted and gave in to the kiss and answered back with the same intensity he showed her.

He kept her arms above her head with one hand and pushed up her T-shirt with his other. She gasped as he moved his mouth to her cloth-covered nipple.

His mouth was hot and wet, his tongue teasing, and he lightly scraped her nipple with his teeth. She gave in completely and barely realized he had let her arms go as he moved his mouth to her other breast.

He rose and tugged her T-shirt up, yanked it over her head, and laid it over the rock he'd been sitting on. He reached beneath her and unfastened her bra and pulled it away from her. The air was cool on her nipples and she felt an amazing sense of wickedness at being bare outside on the range.

After he tossed the bra aside to land on top of the blouse on the rock, he moved over her and braced one hand to the side of her head.

"Are you going to be good?" His expression was dark and intent as he reached between them and unfastened her belt. "You know what I'll do if you aren't."

She swallowed. She could fight him and she knew he'd catch her and punish her all over again. That thought sent another thrill through her and she was tempted to struggle just to be manhandled by him. But at the same time she didn't want to fight him anymore. She wanted whatever he would give her.

He brushed his lips over hers. "Are you going to fight me?"

She shook her head. "No."

His smile was slow and sensual and he eased down her body. He knelt at the foot of the blanket and watched her as he took one of her boots in his hands and slipped it off before setting it aside. He took off the other boot before removing her socks and stuffing them into the boots.

He moved closer again and pulled her belt out of the loops and unbuttoned her jeans. As soon as her zipper was down, he tugged off her jeans and stripped them away, leaving her only in her black panties. It only took a moment for him to slip those off, too. He put her panties and jeans on top of her other clothing.

He tugged at her nipple. "I want to eat you up like you ate that ice cream in Scottsdale. It was so damn hot watching you."

She swallowed, feeling suddenly shy and nervous. She started to put her arms over her breasts but he stopped her by catching her wrists in one hand.

"Oh, no you don't." He shook his head. "I want to see you."

He released her then tossed his Stetson onto her clothing before unbuttoning his western work shirt, all the while keeping his gaze fixed on her. The air felt cool on her body and her nipples were impossibly tight. She swallowed as she watched him remove his clothing, piece by piece, from his boots and socks to his belt.

Excerpt... Playing With You

Cheyenne McCray

The moment they walked in the door to Ricki's home, Garrett slammed the door hard behind him and grabbed her up in his arms. He grasped her ass and pressed her hard against him as his mouth took hers.

A shiver went through her that had nothing to do with her soaked clothing, and everything to do with the way he was kissing her. It was hungry and almost harsh, his lips bruising hers.

She responded with her own hunger for him, wrapping her arms around his neck and pressing herself as close to him as she could, even closer than he already had her. His cock was so hard against her belly that it sent a thrill through her, straight to that place between her thighs. She'd never wanted a man like she wanted Garrett, and she was finally going to have him.

The next thing she knew, her head was spinning as he took her down to the floor and onto a thick rug in the entryway. His baseball cap dropped to the rug as he kissed her, and she hooked her thighs around his hips as he pressed his jean-clad cock against her center. She squirmed beneath him as she moaned with need.

They were still coated with mud, their clothing soaked through. She didn't care if he took off his clothes—she just wanted to feel him inside her as soon and as fast as possible.

"Damn, but you're fine." He pushed up her T-shirt, grabbed her red bra, and jerked it below her large breasts. "I've got to have you."

She gasped as cool air tightened her nipples and then his warm mouth latched onto her. He thrust his hips as if taking her, his cock rock hard against her through their clothing.

Desire and need coursed through her and she whimpered to be even closer to him. She moved both of her hands down between them and fumbled until she unbuttoned his jeans. She slid her hand into the waistband of his jeans and his underwear, and wrapped her fingers around his cock.

He groaned and moved his hips as she eased her hand up and down his length. He was thick and long and she gave another soft moan, imagining how it would feel once his cock was inside her.

"Garrett." She sighed his name as she begged him. "Please."

His mouth found hers again and his muscular chest pressed against her chest, his T-shirt abrading her bare nipples. Her eyes were closed as she became lost in the kiss, loving the way he was taking control and the unleashed power he was exerting over her.

He stilled, then moved his mouth from hers as he pulled back. She opened her eyes and found him looking down at her with pain and anger in his expression, his hands braced to either side of her head.

Confused, she furrowed her brow. "What's wrong, Garrett?"

He didn't answer. Instead he pushed himself to his knees between her thighs, pulled her bra back over her breasts and tugged down her T-shirt. He got to his feet and taking her by the hands, brought her up with him.

The anger in his expression almost frightened her. "I'm sorry, Ricki." He released her hands and took a step back as he fastened his jeans. "I shouldn't have touched you."

Her mind was still reeling from his kisses and the feel of his body against hers. "Did I do something wrong?"

"I did." He turned and took the two steps from the entryway rug to the front door. He grasped the door handle, lowered his head, and paused for a moment. Then he straightened, and without looking at her again, he jerked open the door. He walked through the opening and closed the door solidly behind him.

ABOUT CHEYENNE

New York Times and *USA Today* bestselling author Cheyenne McCray's books have received multiple awards and nominations, including

RT Book Reviews magazine's Reviewer's Choice awards for Best Erotic Romance of the year and Best Paranormal Action Adventure of the year

*Three "RT Book Reviews" nominations, including Best Erotic Romance, Best Romantic Suspense, and Best Paranormal Action Adventure.

*Golden Quill award for Best Erotic Romance

*The Road to Romance's Reviewer's Choice Award

*Gold Star Award from Just Erotic Romance Reviews

*CAPA award from The Romance Studio

Cheyenne grew up on a ranch in southeastern Arizona. She has been writing ever since she can remember, back to her kindergarten days when she penned her first poem. She always knew one day she would write novels, hoping her readers would get lost in the worlds she created, just as she experienced when she read some of her favorite books.

Chey has three sons, two dogs, and is an Arizona native who loves the desert, the sunshine, and the beautiful sunsets. Visit Chey's website and get all of the latest info at her website (http://www.cheyennemccray.com) and meet up with her at Cheyenne McCray's Place on Facebook (https://www.facebook.com/CheyenneMcCraysPlace)!

CPSIA information can be obtained at www.ICGtesting.com
Printed in the USA
LVOW11s1655151213

365395LV00021B/2483/P